She had marshmal

Before Farrell could ~~...~~ d
and licked away the ~~...~~
he said huskily.

Her eyes widened. "I didn't understand you at first.
I thought you were a serious scientist devoted to his
work. But you're really a renegade, aren't you?
A hedonist. A rascal."

Farrell gave her a lazy smile. "Isn't it possible to
be all those things? Can't I want to sleep with a
fascinating woman in my spare time?"

She reached out and covered one of his hands with
hers. Her smile was shy. "I hope there won't be much
sleeping involved. Surely we can do better than that."

His heart rate jumped. He twined his fingers with hers.
"Don't toy with me, woman. I need an unambiguous
answer. Do you want to go to bed with me? Here?
Tonight?"

* * *

Upstairs Downstairs Temptation by Janice Maynard
is part of the The Men of Stone River series.

Dear Reader,

Farrell and Ivy have both been hurt by love. But they are so perfect for each other, I promise!

For each of them, falling in love again is out of the question. Each is very happy alone, or as happy as they can be under the circumstances. Life is safer that way.

I hope you enjoy this tale of two people who try their best to go it alone but find out that two hearts are better than one.

Happy reading,

Janice

JANICE MAYNARD

——

UPSTAIRS DOWNSTAIRS TEMPTATION

Recycling programs for this product may not exist in your area.

ISBN-13: 978-1-335-20915-3

Upstairs Downstairs Temptation

Copyright © 2020 by Janice Maynard

For questions and comments about the quality of this book, please contact us at CustomerService@Harlequin.com.

Harlequin Enterprises ULC
22 Adelaide St. West, 40th Floor
Toronto, Ontario M5H 4E3, Canada
www.Harlequin.com

Printed in U.S.A.

Books by Janice Maynard

Harlequin Desire

Southern Secrets

Blame It On Christmas
A Contract Seduction
Bombshell for the Black Sheep

Texas Cattleman's Club: Inheritance

Too Texan to Tame

The Men of Stone River

After Hours Seduction
Upstairs Downstairs Temptation

For Ainsley.

You're smart and creative,
and you always make me laugh!
I love you bunches...

One

Farrell Stone didn't like asking for help. Rarely would he do so when it came to business, and even less in his personal life. He went his own way. Handled his own affairs. Kept his own counsel.

Unfortunately, his administrative assistant, Katie, was a pro at butting in…which was why he now found himself in the midst of this odd interview with Katie's protégée.

The woman who sat quietly across the desk from him was thin and not too tall. Barely five-three, perhaps. Her thick, shiny hair, the color of rich chocolate, was cut short in choppy layers that emphasized her pointed chin.

Huge, long-lashed eyes seemed too big for her face. The expression in her wary feminine gaze was equal parts fearful and hopeful. Hazel irises sparkled with flecks of gold and green.

Though she was not traditionally beautiful, there was something compelling about her. Farrell was drawn to her soft femininity and her almost palpable aura of vulnerability. She was exactly the kind of woman he found sexually appealing. The fact that he felt a flutter of physical response alarmed him.

He had trained himself to ignore sexual need. Now was not the time to break that habit.

Though she was originally from here in Maine, Ivy Danby had spent most of the last two decades in South Carolina. The résumé in Farrell's hand was so slim as to be nonexistent. Graduated high school. Worked a handful of jobs. Married. Then nothing. Although the fact that the woman held a sleeping baby in her arms pointed to a few details that might have been omitted.

He dropped the single sheet of paper and drummed his fingers on his desk. "I appreciate you coming in for an interview, Ms. Danby, but—"

She leaned forward urgently, taking him by surprise. Halting his polite brush-off. "Whatever you need me to do, I can learn," she said. She stared at him, unblinking. As if sheer determination could manipulate him.

He liked her confidence, but with every minute that passed, he became more sure that he didn't need the complication of being attracted to an employee.

The woman's voice was husky and slow as honey in winter. *Whatever you need me to do...* It was only Farrell's surprisingly naughty libido that added the sexual subtext.

It irked him that he wasn't entirely ready for this

conversation. But opportunity had come knocking, as they say. He sighed. "I haven't advertised for this position. You understand that, right?"

Ivy nodded. "I do. But your administrative assistant, Katie, apparently knows something is coming available. And she also knows I need a job. I'm currently sharing an apartment with her sister."

Farrell rubbed the center of his forehead with two fingers, trying to stave off a headache. "My admin is now my sister-in-law. She and my brother Quin were married three months ago."

The woman lifted an eyebrow. "And she still comes to work every day?"

The question struck Farrell as odd. "I think Quin assumed she might quit. But Katie is very much her own person. She likes running the R & D department. I honestly don't know what I would do without her."

Ivy Danby nodded. "I've only met her once, and it was a wonderful conversation. She's an amazing person."

"That she is." Farrell hesitated. "Here's the thing, Ivy. The job is in the middle of nowhere in northern Maine."

She blinked. "Oh."

Farrell was an engineer. An inventor. Traditionally, he had worked from his state-of-the-art lab here in this building in Portland…on this floor. In the past twenty-four months, though, he had seen his best and newest ideas pop up in the marketplace before he had a chance to get them there.

Though it was possible he was paranoid, the prospect of corporate espionage was something he couldn't rule out.

"My brothers and I each own homes on the northern coast," he said. "I've recently built a small lab and a guesthouse on my property. As soon as possible, I'm going to move my work up there."

"Do you mind me asking why?"

"Aspects of my designs are highly confidential. I've decided I need to be more vigilant in protecting my research. Not only that, but I like being on my own, and I work best in solitude."

"Then why does Katie think you need to hire someone?"

He grimaced and ran his hands through his hair. "I'm single-minded when I'm in the midst of a project. I've been known to work for thirty-six hours straight if I'm in the zone. I need someone to run my house and prepare meals. Particularly a person who can be discreet and trustworthy."

An odd expression flashed through her eyes. Something dark. Something that surprised him.

"I can keep my mouth shut, Mr. Stone. I can keep secrets."

Finally, he asked the question he'd been putting off. "Why would you want a job like this, Ivy? We have internet and TV up north, but nothing else. Not even a convenience store nearby."

Was it his imagination, or did she clutch the baby more tightly? For the first time, she revealed agitation. Anxiety.

"I have to be honest with you," she said.

That sexy voice affected him in ways he couldn't explain. "Please do."

Her bottom lip trembled the slightest bit. Her eyes sheened with moisture. "I'm desperate, Mr. Stone. My husband died a few months ago. He left me nothing. No life insurance. Nothing. The house was sold, and the money went elsewhere. My parents are gone. I have no other family. I need a job where I can have Dolly with me."

"Dolly?"

Ivy stroked her baby's head. "Dorothy Alice Danby. That's a mouthful, so Dolly for short." Ivy paused. Stared at him with an intensity that took him off guard. "I know you don't remember me from our childhood. We were at the same elementary school. But everybody in Portland knows your family—your father, your brothers, Zachary and Quinten. Stone River Outdoors provides hundreds of good jobs. I'm only asking for a chance. I'm a hard worker. And the baby still takes two long naps every day. I also have an infant carrier, so she can stay on my back while I'm cooking or cleaning. If you hire me, I swear you won't regret it."

Ruefully, Farrell realized he was regretting it already. His life needed fewer complications, not more. As far as he could tell, Ivy Danby with her artless sex appeal and her tiny daughter was a whole huge bundle of complications.

With an inward sigh, he admitted defeat. "You make a compelling argument. But for the record, I do remember you, Ivy. We were both in Mrs. Hansard's third-grade class together. You had pigtails. Your desk was in the row beside mine two seats back. I gave you a valentine that year. One I made myself."

Her eyes widened, and her cheeks flushed. "Oh," she said. "You do remember."

"Give me twenty-four hours to think about it. I'll call you tomorrow and let you know what I've decided."

He saw on her face that she wanted an answer right now. Wanted it badly, in fact. But she swallowed the protest on her lips and managed a wobbly smile. "I understand. Thank you for the interview."

As soon as his guest departed, Farrell stabbed a button on his intercom and barked an order. Moments later, Katie Duncan Stone appeared in his doorway. The blue-eyed blonde was both beautiful and competent. She was also stubborn and dogged about helping people, whether they deserved it or not.

Farrell folded his arms across his chest and glared. "Really, Katie? A new mom with a baby?"

"Don't be so sexist, Farrell Stone." She took the comfy seat at his desk that Ivy had recently vacated. "New moms can work."

"If they have access to childcare. My house is in the woods on a cliff above the ocean." He ground his teeth, haunted by the memory of entreaty in Ivy's hazel-eyed gaze, but even more disturbed by how very much he wanted to say yes to this idea.

Katie visibly dismissed his protest. "A hundred years ago, regular women didn't have childcare. But they worked their asses off. It can be done."

"Why are you pushing this so hard?" His brother Quin had warned him about Katie's penchant for rescuing humans and the occasional animal, too. She had a huge heart.

"I met Ivy when I dropped by my sister's apartment over on Kimball Street the other day. In conversation, we realized that you and Ivy were in school together."

"*Elementary* school," Farrell said with a sigh. "That's hardly a character reference."

His new sister-in-law was not to be deterred. "Ivy moved in with nothing, Farrell. No furniture. No belongings. She had two suitcases, a port-a-crib and a diaper bag. Nothing else. Don't you think that's kind of strange?"

"Maybe, maybe not."

"She's hurting. And alone. Surely you, of all people, can sympathize. Losing a spouse changes your whole world."

Farrell took the hit stoically. Only Katie would have the guts to bring up his past. It had been seven years since Sasha died. Even his own brothers didn't go there. "Dirty pool," he muttered.

Katie stood and kissed him on the cheek. "You and I are family now. I get to meddle. But in this instance, I'm begging you, Farrell. Ivy Danby needs a fresh start. She needs a home and security. She needs exactly what you have to offer. Please give her a chance."

Ten days after the uncomfortable interview at Stone River Outdoors headquarters in Portland, Ivy found herself in an expensive luxury sedan being driven north by Katie Stone, herself.

Ivy had been shocked when the big boss contacted

her. In a terse, four-minute conversation, Farrell Stone had offered her the job and a salary that made her eyes bug out. Katie called soon afterward to outline the specifics. As Farrell's admin, Katie knew what would be required of Ivy. She also knew that Ivy had no car, no furniture and no money.

Katie had a solution for every problem. She insisted she needed to check on her husband's house, now hers also, and thus it would be no trouble at all to take Ivy and Dolly to their new home.

The trip had been pleasant so far. Dolly babbled and played in the back. When she became fussy, Katie found a rest area and pulled off so Ivy could prepare a bottle for the baby, get Dolly out of her car seat and feed her comfortably.

They rolled down the windows and enjoyed the pleasant breeze. Katie's gaze was wistful. "I want to have kids," she said softly. "I don't know if my husband is ready, though."

Ivy cradled Dolly's cheek. "You haven't been married long. There's plenty of time."

"I know," Katie said. "But that biological clock you hear about is ticking loudly." She flicked at a mosquito that tried to enter the car. "How did you know you wanted kids?"

Ivy stiffened, keeping her eyes locked on her daughter. "I didn't," she said. "It just happened."

"Ah, well, I guess you were one of the lucky ones."

"I suppose." Ivy's throat was tight. She let the silence build, knowing she had to keep it together. Crying over the past at this stage in the game might cost her this precious job. "She's had enough," she said, gently loosening the baby's lock on the nipple. Dolly's mouth and tiny tongue still made little sucking motions, but her head lolled back. "We can get on the road."

Katie grinned. "Ah, to be that young and innocent again."

While Ivy tucked Dolly back into her car seat, Katie visited the restroom and then Ivy took her turn. Soon, they were driving north again. For so long, Ivy had kept her emotions in lockdown mode. But today, of all days, she had reason to smile. She was headed to a job and a place to live and a salary that would support her tiny family. On this warm autumn day with the sunshine beaming down and the skies a brilliant blue, a tiny sprout of hope unfurled.

Birches, oaks and maples put on a fantastic display of color. Vibrant reds and orangey golds…deep yellows and every shade of brown. Mother Nature had outdone herself this season.

Maybe by next year Ivy would have the opportunity and the financial means to explore this area with her daughter. The prospect seemed like a really wonderful fantasy.

She shook herself inwardly. Grief had stolen her hopes and dreams, but that was in the past. She was rebuilding her life, reinventing who she was. Nothing was beyond her reach if she believed in Ivy Danby.

The fact that Farrell Stone was the author of her good fortune gave her pause. She liked him. A lot. He was honorable and handsome and sexy in a gruff, understated kind of way.

She honestly thought her life experiences had erased her ability to feel like a woman. But when she sat across the desk from Farrell, she found herself wanting more than a job. Maybe a smile. A shared laugh.

She would have to be very careful not to make a fool of herself.

Ivy had plenty to think about as Katie concentrated on the traffic. In Bangor, they merged south and east onto the narrower 1A toward Bar Harbor. At Ellsworth, just before the crowded tourist playground that included Acadia National Park, they turned onto a less traveled road for the last leg to Stone River.

Here, nobody but locals traversed the winding rural highway. Nothing much to see but acres of forest and fields and peaceful ponds and lakes. The pastoral scenery soothed some of Ivy's apprehensions.

Katie glanced at the clock on the dash. "Not much longer now. Can you tell we're near the ocean?"

"Actually, yes. Living in Charleston for so long taught me the smell and feel of the air at the coast. It's not as warm or humid here, but I remember the northern sea from my childhood."

"It's just beyond those trees. In the other direction, north and west of us, is the Moosehorn National Wildlife Refuge. And of course, north and east, if you keep going, is the Canadian border."

Ivy had never been this far up in Maine, but in Farrell's office she had seen aerial photographs of three spectacular homes on rocky promontories overlooking the sea, each one bearing the stamp of its owner.

Almost two centuries before, a Stone ancestor had

acquired an enormous tract of pristine wilderness. He named the small river meandering through his property after himself. Subsequent generations sold off the bulk of the land, but the current Stone brothers still owned several hundred square miles. They liked their privacy. The company that had made them all wildly wealthy was born in this forested paradise.

The isolation and seclusion weren't daunting to Ivy at all. They represented safety and security. A chance to finally be herself.

When Katie turned off onto the road that accessed Stone family property, she entered a code at the gate and kept right on going. A perfectly paved road meandered for the next seven miles.

Dolly was beginning to stir when they reached Farrell's house. On the way, they had passed turnoffs leading to homes Zachary and Quin had built. "I'll show you our place another day," Katie said. "I know you probably want to get settled in. Shall we go to the big house first and see Farrell, or head straight for the cabin?"

"Cabin, please."

As they wound around the side of Farrell's magnificent house, Ivy craned her neck to get a better view. The place was huge, easily six thousand square feet. Maybe more. It had a traditional New England look to it with lots of blue clapboard and white trim, and even a widow's walk at the very top. Windows everywhere offered views of the ocean.

Behind Farrell's home, deeper into the woods, sat a charming dollhouse of a cabin, constructed of rough-hewn logs. It was perfect in every way, and when Ivy stepped out of the car and inhaled, the scent of freshly cut wood assailed her nose.

"This is it," Katie said, looking over the top of the car at Ivy. "Do you think you and Dolly will be comfortable here?"

Ivy wanted to laugh incredulously. The setting was sheer wonder. "Who wouldn't be?" she said calmly. "It looks perfect."

The inside was even better than the outside. The cabin was small, barely eight hundred square feet. Two neat bedrooms with a shared bath between. A compact kitchen with the latest appliances. And a comfy living room with a couch, two matching armchairs and a real wood-burning fireplace.

Someone—Farrell, maybe—had stacked a neat pile of firewood near the hearth. A wooden crate filled with kindling and a mason jar of matches flanked the opposite side.

Ivy felt tears burn her eyelids. She held them back by sheer force of will. Katie wouldn't understand, and Ivy didn't have it in her to explain. Not now. Not today. Maybe not ever.

"Who got the baby bed for us? Was it you?" Ivy asked.

Katie shook her head. "No. That was Farrell's idea. He thought you could leave the port-a-crib at his place, so you'd be able to nap Dolly in either location. That's an engineer for you. Always studying and planning."

"It was very thoughtful." Actually, the magnitude of the gesture spoke volumes about the kind of man

Farrell Stone was. Ivy was overwhelmed and trying not to show it.

Dolly began to fuss, so Ivy opened the back door of Katie's car. "Don't cry, sweet girl. I know it's time to get out." The novelty of the great outdoors soothed the baby's grievances immediately.

Katie laughed. "Look at her face. I think she likes it here."

It was true. The baby's head swiveled from side to side, taking it all in. She stuck her fist in her mouth and sucked it contentedly.

Ivy took a deep breath, searching for composure, gathering herself. "I don't want to keep you too long," she said. "You've already done so much. If it's okay with you, let's go on to the other house so your brother-in-law can show me around and tell me his routine."

Two

Farrell was nervous. The emotion was such an anomaly, he examined it to see if it was actually hunger or fatigue in disguise.

Nope. He was nervous.

Perhaps it was because he was upending his entire working life. Maybe he was afraid the new digs wouldn't be as conducive to creativity as his old lab in Portland.

Or maybe he was still anxious about the possibility of espionage. Was that it? Was he worried about losing another design?

He was a man of measured thoughts and actions. Neither as reckless as his younger brother nor as carefree as his middle brother. Farrell was the oldest. The responsible one.

After examining and discarding all the possible sources of his unease, he came to the only remaining conclusion.

He was nervous about having Ivy Danby move in with him.

Ah, hell. She wasn't moving in with him. He paced the length of the living room, gazing out the huge windows, trying to draw comfort from the ever-changing ocean.

Ivy Danby was going to prepare his meals and clean his house. She and her daughter would *not* be guests beneath his roof. They had another roof. Their own roof.

One that belongs to you, said his annoying inner voice.

Farrell had spotted Katie's car in the driveway almost half an hour ago. Clearly, she was showing Ivy the cabin and helping her settle in. They would be here soon.

When the doorbell finally rang, he ran his hands through his hair and opened the door, hoping he didn't look as rattled as he felt. "Hello, Katie," he said. "And Ivy. Come in."

Dolly stared at him as if he had sprouted a second head. What did Farrell know about kids anyway? Zip. Nada.

So he focused on the two adult women. "Was the trip okay?"

Katie waved a breezy hand. "Piece of cake. They finished that construction on I-95, so we made great time."

"Good. Good."

She eyed him strangely. "I have the last two boxes

of your files in my trunk. I think that's everything you need."

During the past four days, his two brothers and Katie had helped him pack up his lab. There had been confusion in the Portland office. No one but his immediate family knew why he was making this change. He still wondered if it was necessary, but time would tell.

Katie took charge of the awkward moment. "Why don't I play with this cute little munchkin while you two talk?"

When she walked out of the room, Ivy stared at Farrell with those big eyes. He cleared his throat. "I suppose we could start in the kitchen."

Ivy nodded soberly. "Of course."

He showed her the fridge and the pantry and how the cupboards were organized. All things an intelligent grown woman could have figured out on her own. Then he shrugged. "I'm not hard to please. I set the coffee maker the night before, so you don't have to worry about that. I usually work from six a.m. to eight and then take a break for breakfast. I like everything except oatmeal. No oatmeal, please."

For the first time, a little smile tilted Ivy's lips. "Oatmeal is good for your heart," she said.

He scowled. "My heart is fine. No oatmeal."

She saluted him. "No oatmeal. Got it, Mr. Stone."

"You'll have to call me Farrell."

It was her turn to frown. "Why?"

Her stubbornness frustrated him. "Because it's only going to be the two of us up here, and we knew each other years ago, damn it."

Ivy eyed him with disapproval. "There are *three* of us," she reminded him, her voice tart. "And I don't want you cursing around my impressionable daughter. If that's a problem, you can fire me now."

He gaped at her, his normally placid temper igniting. "Seriously? Damn, woman, you're uptight."

"That's number two," she said primly.

In all honesty, he hadn't realized that he had cursed at her a second time. He felt his face get hot. "I will be careful around your daughter."

Ivy gnawed her lip. "Are you a volatile man, Farrell?"

"Volatile?" His jaw dropped again. Never in his life had he been described as volatile. Stubborn, maybe. Too focused when he was working. Emotionally closed off. But never volatile.

Farrell swallowed his frustration and moderated his voice. "I promise you, Ivy, most people think of me as easygoing. I do get lost in my projects at times. It's possible I might forget you're here. But ours will be an even-keeled working relationship. I swear it." *As long as I pretend she's not the most fascinating woman I've met in years.* "I'll go talk to my sister-in-law and let you familiarize yourself with the kitchen."

He found Katie on the front porch showing Dolly the squirrels in the yard. When she spotted Farrell, she smiled. "We're staying in the shade. I doubt Miss Dolly has on sunscreen."

Farrell lowered his voice. "So what's Ivy's deal, Katie? How long ago did her husband die? Did he see his kid born? What happened?"

Katie sobered. "Her private life isn't any of our business, Farrell. The truth is, she won't be gossiping about *your* work. She's in a difficult place, and you're giving her a chance to start over. Delanna said it sounded like Ivy had come from a bad situation, though details were vague. As shell-shocked as Ivy was, she didn't have a lot to say."

"How is your sister these days? Isn't she pissed that you snatched up her roommate and spirited her away?"

"A little. She'll get over it. There'll be another roommate. Now that she ditched her loser boyfriend, Delanna is doing great. She doesn't even ask to borrow money anymore. I'm proud of her." Katie smoothed the baby's hair and kissed the top of her head. She held out her arms. "Do you want to hold her? She's a sweetie pie, aren't you, love?"

Farrell took the baby automatically, only to find that she weighed a lot less than he'd expected. Her little body was warm and pudgy, her skin soft and scented with good baby smells. His heart flopped in his chest. He'd never agonized over not being a father. It wasn't meant to be. But for a fleeting second, he felt a moment's pity for the poor bastard who had died without getting to see his daughter grow up.

He rubbed the baby's back absently. The autumn breeze was cool, but not cold. The day was perfect. "Thank you, Katie," he said, giving his sister-in-law a grateful smile.

She stretched her arms over her head, staring out at the panorama of colorful fall foliage and brilliant blue ocean. "For what?"

"For bringing Ivy to me and helping her get settled, but mostly for making Quin happy."

Katie's small smile was happy, too, and maybe a bit smug. "Did he tell you we're going skiing in December? Nothing major. Just a few runs at Aspen. So he can find his mojo again. And plenty of nights by the fire with hot buttered rum and—"

Farrell held up a hand in alarm. "I don't want to hear about your sexual escapades with my brother."

"How do you know that's what I was going to say?" She grinned.

Farrell chuckled. "You know, Katie, I'm actually looking forward to working in this unorthodox arrangement. A brand-new lab... I may come up with a few brilliant designs."

"I hope you do," Katie said. "Stone River Outdoors needs a boost. These last few years have been hard."

"Yes. They have." He handed the child back to Katie.

His sister-in-law gave him a wry look as if she knew exactly how unwilling he was to bond with the baby. "What did you do with Ivy?"

"She's getting her bearings in the kitchen. I'm sure she'll come find us shortly."

Ivy opened the huge built-in wall refrigerator and stared. Someone had stocked it well. She wondered how far afield she would have to go to replenish perishables, but then she spotted a delivery-service notepad on a corner of the beautiful gray-and-silver-quartz countertop. Apparently, Farrell could get deliveries whenever he liked.

This kitchen was a dream. Ivy was a good cook. She'd had plenty of time to practice over the years with a demanding spouse. Preparing meals here would be no hardship. Farrell's house was like something off one of those HGTV shows. The "after" version on steroids. She knew the Stone family was wealthy, but this was something else again.

More to the point, this was Farrell's *second* home. He owned a large condo in Portland that was probably even swankier than this. She couldn't imagine having that kind of money.

For Ivy's part, she only wanted enough to care for her daughter and keep a roof over their heads. As long as Farrell Stone needed to work in a secret lab deep in the forest, she was determined to make herself indispensable to him.

The kitchen door swung open. The object of her thoughts strode in looking like the alpha male he was. Masculine. In charge. Gorgeous. On his heels was Katie.

Farrell smiled. "Everything okay?"

"More than okay," Ivy said. "This kitchen is amazing." She took Dolly from Katie. "But what about cleaning? How often do you want me to give the whole house a once-over?"

"I can answer that," Katie said. "Men are clueless about these things. Farrell entertains fairly often, at least once a month. Primarily business functions. The top two floors have four bedrooms each, all with their own small en suites. I'm sure you'll want to do a bit of touch-up if there's an event on the calendar. Other than that, you shouldn't have to bother with upstairs until the guests depart."

Farrell frowned. "I can call in a cleaning service after we have a big house party. That shouldn't fall to Ivy. We agreed on meal preparation and *light* housekeeping."

Ivy bristled. "I can handle it."

"No." Farrell's brows drew together in a frown. "That's my decision. Not yours."

She opened her mouth to protest, but he stared her down. "Fine," she muttered. "Waste your money if you want to."

Farrell was an imposing male. His size and visible strength might have unnerved her if she hadn't been so aware of him in a shivery, fascinated way. Besides, he seemed to downplay the fact that he could probably bench-press three hundred pounds.

He topped six feet by several inches. Katie, standing near him, was tall for a woman. Five-eight, maybe. Beside Farrell, she looked positively petite.

Farrell's hair was an intriguing mix. Dark brown like Ivy's, but his was streaked with caramel and gold, a color many women would pay high dollar to achieve. He wore it long enough to be casual, but short enough to fit in with his role as one of the bosses.

His eyes were an odd shade of green, and like his hair—streaked with gold. They were eyes that held a wealth of life knowledge. He seemed a serious man. Grounded. Not prone to whimsy.

That was fine with Ivy. She didn't want any surprises.

Katie glanced at her watch. "I've gotta run," she said. "Have to be back in Portland by six."

The two women hugged. Katie kissed Dolly's forehead. Ivy felt a stab of panic that her benefactor was leaving. "Thank you for all your help, Katie. I appreciate it more than you know."

"Not a problem. I love it up here. Quin and I may head this way sometime soon. I'll see you then."

Farrell left the kitchen to follow his sister-in-law out to her car…like a good host. Or maybe he was simply unloading the boxes of files Katie had mentioned. Ivy lingered behind, pondering the dinner options. This first meal might be tricky. Learning to work in someone else's kitchen was always a challenge. Everyone organized cabinets and drawers differently. She opened the pantry again, and then peeked in the freezer.

Moments later, Farrell returned, his hair tousled from the breeze. "Why don't you and Dolly spend the rest of the afternoon getting to know your new home? I'll throw something together for dinner tonight."

Ivy's eyes widened. It was her turn to stand her ground. "No," she said. "No, Farrell. You hired me to do a job. I appreciate your hospitable nature, but I'll be the one cooking. Is six okay?"

He folded his arms across his chest, his expression telegraphing his displeasure. "I sense that you and I may have the occasional run-in. Do you agree?"

"I don't need your charity. I want to work for my living."

"And yet your résumé had not a single scrap of job

experience listed in the previous ten years. Would you care to explain?"

She sucked in a sharp breath, not expecting him to go on the attack. Her jaw trembled despite her best efforts to steady it. "No," she said quietly. "I wouldn't." She gnawed her lip, trying not to slide into despair. *Fight, Ivy. Fight for yourself and Dolly.* "Have you changed your mind about me?" she asked, her throat dry and tight.

His gaze was puzzled. Concerned. Frustrated. "The job is yours," he said bluntly. "I don't go back on my word. But I also expect my employees to follow my direction."

"Don't you mean your *orders*?" she snapped, horrified the moment the words left her mouth. She closed her eyes briefly and grimaced. "I'm sorry. I know I'm not making the best first impression." She hesitated, for the first time feeling the tsunami of exhaustion that always follows substantive change. "I appreciate your consideration. Dolly will be wanting a nap, and I could use one, too. Please let me know when to return for dinner."

Farrell leaned over the sink and watched his newest employee make her way to the cabin that stood twenty-five yards from the house. *His* new working quarters were housed in a similar structure, just beyond the cabin and to the right.

He had a few hours' grace before he needed to start dinner. But for some reason, he was too unsettled to head out to the lab. It was a perfect spot. The building included a nice office in addition to the lab itself. Today, though, he was off his game. Perhaps it would take time to adjust.

Instead, he went to the porch and carried in the two boxes Katie had brought up from Portland. After dropping them one at a time onto the island in the kitchen, he began to extract files and separate them into the appropriate piles. As he worked, he wondered for the hundredth time how someone had accessed his research and designs.

Was it a cybercrime? Or something as simple as breaking into the building and photographing pieces of paper? Farrell usually did his initial sketches on yellow legal pads. When he was happy with the general idea, he moved everything to an actual design program. He changed his password frequently. Zachary was the only person who knew those passwords, and he memorized them rather than writing them down.

As far as Farrell could tell, Stone River Outdoors was taking normal, prudent precautions in protecting their proprietary intellectual property. Yet somehow, Farrell's last two innovative products had surfaced on the market before he was finished perfecting them. The impostors were substandard. And poorly reviewed online.

But that didn't help the fact that Farrell had labored for months with nothing to show for it. Later, perhaps, in a year or so, he could push his own version of the designs to market. But they wouldn't have the excitement and freshness of a completely new launch.

Carefully, he loaded organized piles back into the boxes. Tomorrow, he would carry them to the lab. In the meantime, he needed to come to terms with Ivy being in his life. Her loss was a painful reminder of his own.

Could he see her day in and day out and not continually think about Sasha? He'd told himself that he was done grieving.

But the heart had its own timetable.

Three

Dolly went to sleep in her new bed as if she had been napping there her whole life. Ivy was desperately glad the baby was so adaptable. Her daughter's short existence had been turbulent at best. Would a tiny child internalize and remember those experiences at a deep level?

Was her psyche permanently damaged?

Was Ivy's?

She shoved aside the dark thoughts. It was a mental exercise she had perfected. Instead of thinking about the past, she took the baby monitor into the second bedroom and set it on the dresser.

Suddenly, she couldn't resist the tempting bed. Exhaustion—mental and physical—was a constant cloak she wore now. Everyone knew that caring for an infant was demanding work. But many new mothers had help. Husbands. Other family members. And not all new mothers dealt with guilt and regret.

Ivy took off her jeans and light cotton sweater and climbed between the covers. She had never slept on anything so soft. The perfect mattress, high-thread-count sheets and heavy, luxurious down-filled comforter were the stuff of dreams.

The Stone family was accustomed to only the best. This "cabin" Farrell had built in the woods was more like a miniature palace. Luxury was imprinted on every item that he, or someone, had selected.

Handmade furniture. Expensive woods. One-of-a-kind paintings on the walls. The cabin might be thematically rustic, but in reality, everything about this little home-away-from-home was exquisite and delightful.

Ivy closed her eyes, thinking about Farrell Stone...

When she awoke an hour and a half later, her heart raced with sudden panic. Dolly. She stumbled to her feet and then sagged against the bed when she saw the image on the monitor. Dolly had clearly just roused from her nap. She was happily playing with her toes and cooing softly. The sweet baby sounds had awakened her mother.

Ivy exhaled slowly, her heart rate slowing to a manageable pace. Everything was okay. She and her baby were safe. It was going to take some time to believe that. She dressed rapidly and prepared a bottle before Dolly went into full temper-tantrum mode. Apparently, the empty-stomach phenomenon was one her daughter embraced.

Sure enough, as Ivy opened the door to the other bedroom, Dolly let out a wail. Ivy scooped her up and smiled. "Don't be such a diva, my love. Mommy is here to feed you." She settled into the gorgeous rocking chair and tucked Dolly against her breast. It was far too soon for the baby to hold her own bottle, but little hands reached out anyway.

Ivy would never get tired of the way Dolly looked up at her with that earnest, wide-eyed expression. "I love you, my sweet girl," she whispered softly. "I think we're going to be happy here." Though financial security and a cozy place to live were the main reasons she could give her daughter that assurance, a little voice inside Ivy's head said that getting reacquainted with the handsome, all-grown-up Farrell would be a bonus.

At a quarter before six, Ivy checked the contents of the diaper bag and then surveyed her own appearance one last time. She hadn't changed clothes. Same faded jeans. Same pink cotton sweater. Farrell had been dressed casually when she met him. He didn't strike her as the kind of man who dressed for dinner when he was in residence at his secluded retreat.

As she gazed in the mirror, she cataloged the evidence of her ordeal. She was too thin. That was something she could work on now that she was settled. Her once shoulder-length waves now barely reached her chin. But that was a good change. Without all the heavy hair, she felt freer. And it was certainly an easier style to care for with an infant demanding her attention.

After finger combing her straight, wispy bangs, and

smoothing her lips with cherry-tinted gloss, she gathered up her daughter and the diaper bag and headed toward the big house. It occurred to her that on rainy or
snowy days, this trek might be problematic with a baby
in tow. She would cross that bridge later.

The stroll was an easy one.

Farrell hadn't given her keys, but the door was unlocked. Presumably, he lived too far in the boonies to
worry about anyone stealing his ideas here.

She entered via a tidy mudroom filled with boots,
coats and fishing gear and proceeded down the hall past
a laundry room, a small guest room and then on to the
kitchen. It wasn't hard to find. She had only to follow
her nose. The smells wafting down the hall were amazing. She realized suddenly that she was starving. She
and Katie had stopped for a fast-food lunch en route,
but that was hours ago.

Farrell looked up when she entered. "Hey, there you
are. I was about to come check on you two ladies."

"We're here. We're good. The naps helped." Farrell's
broad, uncomplicated smile made Ivy's heart kick in
her chest. It had been so long since she had felt anything as pleasurable as sexual arousal, the momentary
jolt of attraction shocked her.

It was normal, she told herself, trying not to overreact. Farrell Stone was a gorgeous, appealing man.
When he returned his gaze to the thick slices of bread
he was smearing with butter, she studied him.

She'd been right not to change clothes. He was still
wearing jeans, too. His moss green pullover stretched to
accommodate broad shoulders. His sleeves were rolled

up. Tanned, long-fingered hands were large and capable, working smoothly.

"It's almost ready," he said, popping the tray of bread in the oven. He paused and grimaced. "I ordered a high chair this afternoon. It will be here tomorrow. I apologize for not thinking of it sooner. In my defense, I'm seldom around babies."

Ivy shook her head. "You didn't have to do that. High chairs are expensive. But I'll pay you back out of my first check."

His cool stare chastised her silently. "No," he said. "You won't. Whatever items you and Dolly need while you're here are simply the cost of doing business. Like a printer or a computer. It's my job to make sure you're comfortable. I've taken you away from civilization. The least I can do is make your stay here as pleasant as possible."

After that, there wasn't much to say. Ivy entertained Dolly. She would have offered to help, but the table in the breakfast nook was already set.

Soon, they were sitting down to steaming plates of angel-hair pasta smothered in meat sauce. The freshly grated Parmesan cheese was a nice touch. And the perfectly browned garlic bread.

Ivy juggled Dolly on one knee and took a bite. "I'm impressed," she said. "This is delicious."

"Don't be." He chuckled. "Mrs. Peterson made the sauce and left it in the fridge. All I did was heat it and throw some pasta in boiling water. Any doofus can do that."

"Mrs. Peterson?"

"Quin's housekeeper. She offered to stock my kitchen and the cabin when she heard I would be working here. In fact, if you ever have any questions, and I'm buried in work, she said for you to feel free to call her."

For a few minutes, they ate without speaking, but the silence made Ivy nervous. "Tell me about your brothers," she said. "I think they're younger than you... Am I remembering that right?"

Farrell stood and topped off their wineglasses with a zinfandel that was smooth and deceptively mild. "Yes. We were stair-steps. Two years apart. You and I are the same age, of course. Then Zachary, then Quin."

"And Quin is the Olympian?"

Farrell nodded. "He was a world-class skier until the accident that claimed our father's life."

"I did know about the wreck. I subscribe to the Portland newspaper online—you know, just to keep up with my old friends. I saw the article and your father's obituary."

"Quin was in the car also. His leg was crushed. He's had multiple surgeries and rehab. He can walk normally now, but competitive skiing is not an option anymore."

"That's awful. He must have been devastated."

"You could say that. We all have moments that change our lives. Fortunately for Quin, Katie came along and helped him pick up the pieces. My baby brother is a new man. A better man, really. Skiing consumed him. He's more balanced now. More at peace with the world."

"And Zachary?"

"Zachary plays the field. I doubt any woman will ever tame him."

Ivy wanted to ask about Farrell's dead wife. She knew he was a widower...nothing more. But if she skated into personal territory with *him*, she would open herself up to questions about her own past. That was not an option, so she ate her spaghetti and kept her curiosity to herself.

Even so, her new boss probed gently. "I know you moved away from Portland a long time ago. What took your family to South Carolina?"

She breathed an inward sigh of relief. This, she could handle. "My dad was a lobster fisherman. But he had aunts and uncles down south. Through one of those connections, he got offered a job as a charter boat captain—taking tourists out for half-day and full-day fishing expeditions. Mom was ready to leave the cold winters, so we packed up and moved. I was twelve, and I wasn't a fan of leaving my friends behind. But it turned out okay."

Ivy could tell he was poised for more questions, so she changed the subject awkwardly. "Will you be coming to the house for your meals, or shall I bring them out to you at the lab? I don't mind. I know you said you can be single-minded when you're working."

He shook his head. "That's far too much trouble. Why don't we compromise? I have a mini fridge in my new office. If you'll make me a sandwich for lunch every morning, I'll take it with me. Then I'll make a point of being back here for dinner at six thirty. Does that work for you?"

Ivy debated rapidly. She normally put Dolly to bed at seven. But she could always nap her a little later and keep her awake until eight. That should be enough time to get the kitchen cleaned up. Especially if she tidied things as she went along. Farrell Stone was being very generous and amenable. She would do her best to fit his schedule and not the other way around.

"Of course," she said. "And please let me know if I prepare foods that are not your favorites. I want you to be satisfied."

He blinked and stood up suddenly.

When she realized how her words had sounded, she was mortified. Though her face must have been bright red, she pretended nothing was wrong for the fifteen minutes it took Farrell to get a carton of ice cream out of the freezer and dish up dessert.

By the time he sat down again, the moment had passed. She hoped.

She ate her ice cream quickly. "Thank you for dinner. If you don't mind, Dolly and I will have an early night. I'll have your breakfast ready at eight tomorrow morning unless you text me otherwise."

Farrell stared at her, his expression impassive. "Relax, Ivy. This isn't a factory job where you'll be punching a clock."

"I know that. But you're paying for a service." Again, unwittingly, she had cast her comment with an ambiguous word choice. She pushed her chair back from the table, feeling jittery and unsure of herself. "Do you mind if we go on back to the cabin?"

"Of course not. Rest well. I never lock the doors here at the house unless I'm gone. We're perfectly safe. But I'll give you a set of keys for the cabin just in case. It's always hard to sleep in a strange place at first. Having everything secured before you go to bed will make you feel better, I'm sure."

He set the two empty ice-cream bowls in the sink and reached in a drawer. "Here," he said. "These are yours."

Ivy took the keys, gripped them in her palm, felt the sharp press of metal and recognized that she had crossed an enormous hurdle. The past was the past. She wouldn't let herself be defined by what had happened to her.

Holding her small daughter, who was all she had left in the world, she smiled up at Farrell Stone, trying not to get emotional. At least not until she could fall apart in private.

"Thank you," she said huskily, her throat tight.

He cocked his head, his emerald-and-amber gaze assessing her. Making assumptions. Trying to dissect her reticence. "You're very welcome, Ivy."

She stood her ground a moment longer, to prove to herself that she could, and then she fled with a muttered goodbye.

Down the hall. Out the door. Into the crisp chill of a New England autumn night. Dolly was sleepy by now. She burrowed into her mother's shoulder, not even protesting the cool air after the warmth of Farrell's kitchen.

Ivy paused in the clearing and looked up at the sky. No moon. In fact, she'd had to pick her way carefully from the house to make sure she stayed on the path. The stars dotted the sky by the billions. Impossibly beautiful. Remote, though. Making Ivy feel small.

She yearned for peace. For happiness. Her dreams were nothing out of the ordinary. Over her life, she had learned valuable lessons. About herself. About the world.

At last, when her skin was chilled, she moved on into the trees and opened the cabin door, then locked it behind her. Though it was childish, perhaps, she checked every room and closet, making sure she and Dolly were alone.

Some people thought the bogeyman was a fictional character. Ivy knew differently.

It had been too long a day to worry about bathing Dolly. Instead, Ivy undressed her and put her in one-piece pajamas and an overnight diaper. Then she fixed a bottle and walked through to the bedroom that would serve as a nursery.

The baby-bed sheet was covered in a tiny circus-animal print. In the drawers she found more bedding and all sorts of infant paraphernalia, including a medium-sized, glossy purple shopping bag on its side. The raffia handles were tied with silver ribbon.

Ivy bent and slid out the gift one-handed. Dolly was getting grumpy, but Ivy wanted to see what was in the fancy sack. Tied to the handle was a note—*I don't have any kids of my own yet, so please let me spoil precious Dolly. Your friend, Katie.*

"Oh, dear," Ivy said aloud, even though Dolly wouldn't understand the words. "What has she done?"

When the contents of the lovely shopping bag were spread out on the bed, Ivy didn't know whether to laugh or cry. No one had hosted a baby shower for her. There had been no work friends to drop by with gifts and food when

Dolly was born. The contrast between then and now was stark. Katie's thoughtful generosity was overwhelming.

Katie had bought Dolly a dozen outfits, half in the size Dolly wore now and half that were the next larger size. The baby clothes were high-end and adorable. Though there were a few pink things, Katie had chosen teal and bright yellow and other vivid colors. Even a miniature designer cardigan that was completely impractical but too cute not to wear.

Ivy took a deep breath. This largesse felt like charity. She hated it when people felt sorry for her. Yet Katie knew none of the specifics of Ivy's life. She merely knew that Dolly was a baby who would grow out of clothes quickly and would need new outfits to wear.

Not only that, but Katie was married to one of the wildly wealthy Stone brothers. This purchase would have been no more than a blip on Katie's platinum credit card.

Before Ivy could overthink it, she picked up her cell phone and pecked out a note, still with one hand. I found the clothes! You are too kind. Dolly and I thank you so much...

By this time, Dolly was no longer willing to wait for her meal any longer. Ivy settled into the rocker. One of Ivy's favorite moments at the end of the day was watching Dolly's beautiful eyelashes settle on her plump, downy cheeks.

The pediatrician recommended putting the baby to bed awake and letting her soothe herself to sleep. But Ivy couldn't give up these precious minutes.

When she climbed into bed later and turned out the

lights, the room filled with unfamiliar shadows. The house settled for the night with creaks and muted pops.

Nothing sinister. Only new surroundings.

As she drifted between waking and sleeping, one image filled her imagination. Farrell Stone. A man she had known literally since childhood. But those words were deceptive. Who knew what kind of human he had become in the intervening years? She remembered a quiet boy. A good student.

Already, those hazy memories were being replaced with new data. Her boss was a full-grown man. Large. Strong. Impressive.

He made her heart beat faster.

God help her...

Four

Farrell dreamed about Sasha. About wandering the hospital halls, unable to find her room. And the doctor who confronted him with sad eyes and said, "She's gone."

He came awake with a start, his heart pounding, his stomach clenched. *Hell.* He thought he was long past this crap. Seven years was plenty of time to grieve, wasn't it?

He rubbed his hands over his face. The alarm would go off in fifteen minutes. Might as well face the day.

The two cups of coffee he swallowed—hot and strong—jump-started his brain. The third serving, in a larger insulated carafe, went with him to the lab. Overhead, birdsong and the sound of the wind in the trees soothed his unease. He walked slowly, feeling his limbs stretch and loosen.

He had to admit, even though he had always been happy working in Portland, this new arrangement had much to commend it. After his father died, he and his brothers had been forced to go from part-time employees to full-time owners in Stone River Outdoors. Little opportunity to stop and smell the roses, or in Farrell's case, the scent of evergreens.

Their father had been a harsh man, but generally fair. He had raised his sons on his own after his wife's death. When the three boys were in their twenties, he hadn't blinked or protested when they wandered the globe sowing their wild oats.

Of course, Farrell had sown fewer oats than the other two. He had married his beloved Sasha young. Been widowed young. After that, he'd been happy to pour most of his energy into research and development for SRO. The company his great-grandfather founded had grown beyond anyone's wildest imagination.

Now Quin was running things, and Zachary had the brains to keep their finances in order. Which left Farrell free to create.

He hadn't realized until this move how much of a routine he had for getting started on his work. Sharpen a few pencils. Straighten his desk. Stare into space, summon the memory of where he had left off.

Now the setting was different. The office layout not the same. But in the end, his methodical approach served him well. In half an hour, he was deep into his latest project.

The next time he surfaced, he glanced at his watch and groaned. Nearly eleven. He'd asked Ivy to have his breakfast ready at eight. She was probably either frustrated or pissed, or both.

He knew he was a hard person to live with. But he didn't want to starve. Or eat peanut butter 24/7. He would assure her he'd do better. Respect her time and effort.

When he rushed into the kitchen, Ivy and Dolly were seated at the island. Ivy wore a simple white cotton button-up top and the same jeans. He knew they were the same, because he'd memorized the rip at one knee.

Ivy had found a set of colorful miniature bowls in his cabinets. The kind of small containers that were good for dipping sauces or individual servings of queso. Dolly had a blue one in her left hand and a green one in her right. The rest were scattered in front of her.

"I'm so sorry," Farrell said. "I promise I'll be on time tomorrow. Maybe set an alarm."

Ivy's expression was noncommittal. "It's your house and your food. You have a right to eat whenever it's good for you."

Something about her careful speech bothered him. "I didn't mean to inconvenience you."

An odd *something* flashed through her eyes. "My job is to have your meal ready when you want it. I've been scrambling eggs every half hour, so they would be warm. The bacon has held up okay." She stood with the baby. "I'll do eggs one more time."

He walked over to the trash can, lifted the lid and stared at the contents. Good God. He turned around to find his new employee watching him warily. He cocked his head. "Weren't you afraid I'd be mad about the wasted food?" He said it jokingly.

Ivy went white. Her mouth opened and closed. "I'm sorry," she muttered. "I'll order more eggs. You can take it out of my check."

She had backed away from him until she was at the farthest point of the kitchen. For one stunned moment, he felt as if he was in a play and didn't know his lines. He'd been hungry before. Starving, actually. But now his appetite fled. "We need to talk," he said slowly. "What kind of man do you think I am?"

She shrugged half-heartedly, clutching the baby as a shield. "I don't know you at all," she said.

He sighed. "I'm the kind of man who won't shout at you if I'm late and the eggs are cold. Are we clear on that?"

A bit of color returned to her face, though her body language still telegraphed her distress. "Okay," she said slowly. "You won't shout. Got it." She paused. "So do I scramble the eggs or not?"

Somewhere, somebody must be laughing at Farrell. He wanted to say *Forget about the damn breakfast*, but he was afraid to upset her. Ivy Danby was fragile. Not in spirit. Not in determination. But she had survived *something*. The hints he was beginning to pick up ate at him.

Should he probe for the truth, or leave her alone to heal on her own?

While he debated how to handle the situation, Ivy cocked her head. "Eggs, Farrell?"

He shrugged and scraped his hands through his hair. "No. I'll grab a sandwich and eat an early lunch." He hesitated. "I may not have been completely honest. I won't shout at you about eggs, but I do sometimes get frustrated. If I *were* to yell, it wouldn't be because I'm upset with you."

This time she stared at him so intently he felt the back of his neck prickle. That steady female gaze got under his skin. Was she always so serious, so focused?

"Do you mean that you have a temper?" she asked.

In another situation, it might have seemed an innocuous question. But to Ivy, it wasn't. He knew that in his gut.

"Doesn't everyone from time to time?" he said lightly, trying to defuse the fraught conversation with humor.

She gnawed her lower lip, a lip that was soft and pink but bore no makeup, not even lip gloss. "No. Not me," she said. "But most people do, I guess."

"There are different kinds of temper," he said gently. "Some people let off steam by being loud. But they don't mean anything by it. They aren't evil or dangerous."

She jerked when he said the word *dangerous*. He saw the slight physical reaction. And he also saw the way she tried to cover up her response.

Too late, Ivy.

"I understand," she said.

Those two words were the biggest lie she had told him. He would have to handle her with care. He was good at caring for people. Sasha told him once it was his love language. But only for her, his wife. Not for any other woman. Sasha had been strong and independent until cancer beat her down.

He cleared his throat. "Why don't you take a look

around the house? Make yourself at home. Nothing is off-limits. I'll throw a sandwich together and get back to the lab."

For the first time, a hint of humor blossomed on Ivy's heart-shaped face. With the short haircut and the big eyes, she looked far younger than he knew her to be. She shook her head slowly. "If I let *you* fix the sandwich, that will be *three* meals I haven't fed you. Hold Dolly. I'll make the sandwich."

Before he could protest, the baby was in his arms, smelling sweetly of lotion and some indefinable infant smell. "How old is she?" he asked abruptly. He could hazard a guess, but suddenly, he wanted to know for sure. Ivy and her little daughter were a puzzle that obsessed him at the moment.

That wary expression came back. Ivy turned to rummage in the fridge, her voice muffled as she took out a package of roast beef and another of Swiss cheese. "Seven months."

He stroked the baby's chubby arm. "So her father got to know her before he passed?"

Ivy straightened and whirled around. "Don't," she said sharply. "Don't do that."

"Do what?"

"Don't try to analyze me, or my life, or Dolly. I'm here to do a job. Nothing more. You and I aren't friends, Farrell."

He chuckled, feeling better suddenly. "So you *do* have a temper, Ivy. Right? It's not a crime."

Her face was the picture of astonishment. Was she really so lacking in self-awareness? Or had she battened down her natural responses for so long that she had forgotten what it felt like to experience true emotions, whether positive or negative?

"I'm sorry I pried," he said. "I'll take Miss Dolly out to the front porch to look at the ocean while you handle things in here."

Ivy fretted as she prepared Farrell's lunch. How could she have been so rude to him? He was paying her a ridiculous amount of money to do a relatively modest amount of work. She should be catering to his every whim, not snapping at him.

But maybe her days of tiptoeing around men were over. She was a grown woman with her own ideas, her own way of doing things. The novelty of that freedom was not something she took for granted.

She added fresh tomato slices and a crisp leaf of lettuce to the thick sandwich and slapped the second piece of bread on top. Since she hadn't actually *cooked* for the man yet, she'd better make sure this lunch was a work of art. After washing an apple and tucking it into one of the brown paper sacks she had found in the cabinet, she added napkins, packaged condiments and the cellophane-wrapped sandwich on top.

Farrell could choose his own drink. The fridge was stocked with bottled sodas, tea and plenty of water. She didn't know his preference.

When the lunch was ready and the kitchen restored to its pristine condition, she made her way through the house to the front door. Pausing by a window, she observed Farrell Stone interacting with her daughter.

He was talking to Dolly, pointing toward the ocean. Though Ivy couldn't hear the exact words, she watched his body language. The infant was secure in his left arm. Her little face was tipped up to his, her smile happy. Contented. The expression on her daughter's face filled Ivy with relief.

Supposedly dogs and babies were good judges of character. If that was true, Farrell Stone was passing the test with ease. Ivy wasn't so easily won over, though. She had learned the hard way that people could present a facade to the world that was entirely false.

Even now, she cringed inwardly as she recalled how easily she had been deceived. Her many missteps and mistakes would haunt her for the rest of her life. More than anything, she wanted to protect Dolly from being as vulnerable as Ivy had been.

Farrell laughed suddenly and kissed the baby on the top of her head. That unscripted bit of affection caught Ivy off guard and twisted her heart. He was so good with Dolly, so natural. Was he really the man he seemed?

With his back to her, she was able to watch him unobserved. Broad shoulders, a powerful torso. The navy Henley shirt he wore revealed bone and muscle. Farrell Stone was intensely masculine. She shivered, caught in something she didn't want to name.

Sexual desire was like an endangered species. She recognized it. Was even drawn to it. But a smart woman would keep her distance.

Farrell must have sensed he was being watched. He turned toward the window, waved and beckoned her to come outdoors. Reluctantly, she joined him. The day was warmer now, much warmer than when she and Dolly had walked over from the cabin.

"Your lunch is ready," she said quietly. Dolly made no move to reach for her mother. Apparently, she was fascinated with her new friend. Dolly's whole world had centered around her mother up until now. It would be good for her to broaden her circle of relationships with adults.

Farrell nodded. "Thanks," he said, keeping his gaze focused on the sea. As they watched, a trio of sailboats danced across the waves on the open water, their sails pure white against the glistening azure water.

"Do you sail?" Ivy asked.

He shot her a sideways glance. "I do. Why? Are you interested in trying it? I'm happy to give you lessons."

She sighed, ignoring his offer. "I'm very sorry I said we weren't friends. That wasn't nice at all."

His smile was a flash of white teeth that sent her stomach into free fall. "I believe in second chances, Ivy Danby. Why don't you and I start over? My name is Farrell, and I'm very happy you're here with me in the Maine woods."

"You are?" She looked up at him, frowning slightly. "That day in your office I got the impression you were hiring me under duress."

His cheeks reddened as if her question had embarrassed him. But that was impossible. Men like Farrell Stone possessed unshakable confidence.

He shrugged. "It's true I prefer to be alone when I work. I'm sorry if I made you feel unwelcome."

She chuckled, almost stunned to feel the jolt of amusement. "I'm not a guest, Farrell. And you haven't made me feel unwelcome. Not at all. You gave me a fabulous place to live, and you bought my daughter a baby bed. I'm in your debt."

"Absolutely not." His frown was dark. "We're even partners in this arrangement, Ivy. Your contributions to this setup are important. I want you to understand that."

"You mean it, don't you?" Staring at him, she searched his brilliant green eyes, the amber bits catching the sun. Could she take him at face value? Did she dare?

"Of course I do," he said. "I have my failings, but I like to think I'm a man of my word."

They were standing so close she could see a tiny spot on the underside of his chin where he had nicked himself shaving. Did he normally shave here in his admittedly luxurious getaway home, or had he done it because Ivy and Dolly were with him?

She held out her right hand. "Starting over is a good idea," she said. "Let's shake on it." That last bit was a mistake. Did she really want to touch the man? Her subconscious said *yes*.

When Farrell took her hand in his much larger one, she sucked in a tiny breath, hoping he hadn't noticed. His grip was firm and warm, telegraphing their mutual accord, but other things, as well.

Ivy was assailed with a dozen feelings she couldn't separate. Relief that he hadn't been irreparably offended by her snit earlier. Amazement that something as simple as a handshake could turn her knees wobbly.

Was Farrell Stone affecting her so deeply because

he had been kind to her daughter? Or was Ivy, herself, desperate to believe that good men still existed? Surely she wasn't so pathetically needy.

The handshake was over far too soon. Farrell let go first. His gaze was inscrutable now, his jaw tight. He handed her the baby. "I need to get back to work," he said gruffly.

"Of course." She swallowed her hurt that he was so eager to rush away. He had come here to make progress on his designs for new Stone River products. Naturally he wanted to focus in his lab.

Ivy was still dealing with the touch of his hand against hers. A touch that felt incredibly good. But she didn't trust her own judgment.

She couldn't. She shouldn't.

More amazing was the fact that she hadn't flinched when their hands came together. His tangible strength hadn't frightened her. Maybe she was making progress.

Five

Farrell was accustomed—when necessary—to concentrating in the midst of distractions. In fact, his ability to shut out peripheral commotion and disturbances was part of what made him good at his job. Creating—inventing—required quiet time and open *space*.

He had plenty of both here in northern Maine. The silence helped him think. The natural beauty of the landscape refreshed his soul.

By all accounts, he should be able to zero in on his goals better than he ever had before. His new digs were an innovator's dream. Now that he was away from the Portland office, he no longer had to worry about some mysterious person stealing his ideas. He was far off the beaten path, and the locals could spot an intruder a mile away.

Yet he found himself far too often staring out the window into the woods, his thoughts scattering in all directions. One of those compass points always landed on Ivy.

She'd been here almost three weeks now. They had fallen into a routine of sorts. As he promised her that very first morning, he had made a point of being on time for breakfast. His meal was always waiting on him when he loped from the lab to the house at eight sharp.

Ivy was a good cook. Excellent, in fact. In his kitchen, with the sun streaming through the windows and the scent of bacon in the air, she always claimed to have eaten earlier when the baby woke up. So Farrell consumed his eggs or his pancakes alone. He checked email on his phone, scrolled through a few *New York Times* articles. Wondered about Ivy.

Dinner took an opposite tack. He had insisted, somewhat doggedly, that Ivy eat her evening meal with him. The high chair he ordered had arrived. The three of them— man, woman and baby—were cozy in the breakfast nook.

Once, when Ivy tried to serve him dinner in the formal dining room with a single place setting of china and silver, he rolled his eyes and carried everything back to the kitchen. After the second night, she gave up.

Never again had he asked about her late husband. He and Ivy had brokered an unspoken accord. He avoided personal questions, and she kept him fed. It was working for now.

What really disturbed him most was the conviction that he was obligated to dig out the truth about her past and help her.

He didn't want to. That reluctance, by all accounts, made him a selfish son of a bitch. When Sasha died, he promised himself never again to get so wrapped up in another woman. The pain of losing his high school sweetheart had turned him into a shell of a man.

Eventually, his world had started spinning again. Sasha's ordeal faded into memory. Time healed all wounds, or so he had been told. Almost imperceptibly, he began to live again. And his life had turned out to be pretty good in many ways.

But intimacy? No, thanks. When sexual hunger drove him beyond what he could handle, he occasionally traveled. Found a woman who was as much of a loner as he was. The two of them enjoyed something strictly physical. It wasn't ideal, but it was all he wanted.

Ivy scared him, because he was attracted to her. She was so very *real*. He wanted to take care of her, and he wanted to *have* her. In his bed.

If he delved into her life, her past, he would get too involved. He might step over the line. Not only for boss/employee, but for his own personal boundaries.

He didn't have the emotional bandwidth to give a woman what she needed.

Or maybe that wasn't true. Maybe he simply didn't ever want to be so vulnerable. He knew what it felt like to lose someone important. He couldn't go through that pain again.

Ivy liked her job. She and Dolly were adjusting well to the new environment. It had taken a couple of days to feel comfortable in Farrell's fabulous kitchen, but even that was easier by the end of the first week.

One Friday morning, she was surprised when Katie showed up out of the blue right after breakfast. She and Farrell put their heads together for an hour about R & D department issues. Then Katie sought out Ivy at the cabin.

The attractive, sexy blonde made Ivy feel inadequate in all sorts of ways. Not on purpose, of course. But Katie was gorgeous. And confident. And blissfully happy as a newlywed. She was also running things back in Portland while Farrell worked here in the middle of nowhere.

When Katie begged to play with the baby, Ivy got Dolly up from her nap and changed her. As Ivy returned to the living room, Katie grinned. "Is it possible she's grown since the last time I saw her?"

"Maybe," Ivy said. "She's healthy and happy here."

Katie cocked her head. "And you?"

Ivy flushed. "Yes. Things are going well."

"Farrell says you cook like a dream."

"I'm glad he thinks so."

"Do the two of you get along?"

"We had a few spats the first couple of days. But we understand each other now."

"Good." Katie gave her a pointed stare. "I need to talk to you about something. But you have to promise not to freak out."

"That's not a reassuring way to start a conversation." Ivy's stomach flipped and flopped. "Is it Farrell? Has he changed his mind? And he's too chicken to tell me himself?"

The last eight words came tumbling out indignantly.

Katie gaped, then laughed. "Farrell Stone is the bravest man I know…after my husband. And no. He hasn't changed his mind. But you know how I mentioned that Farrell entertains often?"

"Yes."

"Well, next weekend is a big event. Farrell and I have been trying to pull it together. But we didn't know until yesterday that it was going to work out. Stone River Outdoors is hoping to partner with a few overseas entities to extend our global reach."

"I see." Ivy told herself not to overreact.

Katie continued. "We have some heavy hitters flying in for a 'summit' here at Farrell's house. A watchmaker from Switzerland. A well-known safari company from Namibia. A couple of ecotour operators from the British Virgin Islands. Plus, a husband and wife who organize walking tours in Tuscany. Farrell, Zachary and Quin are hoping to convince them all to use Stone River products, and in turn, we'll advertise for each of our partners."

"So lots of cooking."

Katie looked guilty. "Not exactly. We're bringing in a professional chef for the weekend. Farrell wants *you* to act as his hostess. My sister has agreed to come with me and babysit Dolly. Here at the cabin, of course. So you won't have to worry about her."

Ivy shook her head, her fists clenching. "Delanna? Oh, no," she said. "That won't work."

"I'll be here the whole time," Katie said. "Except at night. Quin and I will sleep at our place."

"And Zachary? Does he have a significant other? Somebody better suited than me to take over here?"

"Zachary is the quintessential bachelor. He goes where the wind blows him. Although to be fair," she said quickly, "he really *has* curtailed his traveling since Mr. Stone died. Zachary is the financial genius at headquarters. He keeps us in the black. He'll be staying up here, too, but in his own house."

"When you talked to me about this job back in Portland, I thought you meant the occasional dinner party," Ivy muttered. "I'm not who you need. Besides, I don't have the right clothes."

Katie juggled Dolly in one arm and reached into an expensive leather tote. "We're going to take care of that right now." She pulled out a sheaf of catalogs. "I've made a list of everything you'll want. Farrell is paying, of course. If you don't like the colors and styles I've picked, feel free to say so. I've folded down the appropriate pages. We'll do overnight shipping. If there are things that don't fit, that will give us time to do exchanges."

When Katie handed over the catalogs, Ivy looked at them in a daze. Farrell hadn't been kidding about his efficient admin. Katie was a military general, planning… executing. There were dressy pants and tops. Couture negligees. A trio of cocktail dresses. Casual hiking clothes.

Ivy shook her head. "I can't," she said. Her nose

burned and her eyes stung. This was a world she knew nothing about.

Katie read her distress. Her smile was kind. "You can do this, Ivy."

"But I'm not like you." Ivy indicated the glossy catalogs. "I've never worn anything so nice."

The other woman smiled wryly. "You may not know this, but my life before I married Quin was far more blue-collar than black-tie. I *worked* with the Farrell men, but that was as far as it went. Now I'm one of the family. It's been sink or swim. I've had to keep up with their lifestyle, but it's really not as bad as it sounds, Ivy. It's kind of nice being pampered."

Ivy changed course. "I don't even really know your sister."

"You moved in with her."

"For three nights. That's all. She advertised for a roommate."

"She already loves Dolly. And though my sister can be flaky at times, she's great with kids. Plus, as I mentioned, you'll be close by the entire time. Nothing to worry about."

"Why can't you be the hostess?"

Katie's smile was smug. "Because Farrell wants *you*. I'm a newlywed. My husband and I will go home every evening. You'll be on hand to juggle any overnight emergencies."

"Overnight?" Ivy's eyes widened.

For the first time, Katie looked guilty. "Did I forget to mention that? Farrell wants you to stay in one of the guest rooms."

"Why didn't he ask me himself?" Ivy demanded. "This doesn't sound like him at all."

"Well, you'd be wrong, then. He says you're smart and capable, and he thinks you'll be the perfect person to make his guests comfortable."

After that, things snowballed out of Ivy's control. It made sense that Katie was organizing the entire weekend. After all, she had been Farrell's administrative assistant for a long time. What didn't make sense was expecting *Ivy* to jump into a high-octane situation and pretend she moved in these circles.

Over lunch, Farrell added his two cents' worth. "Thank you, Ivy," he said. "Katie tells me she went over all the particulars with you. We'll have barely a week to get ready, but Katie and Quin will fly up Thursday morning to help with final details. Zachary will be in charge of hiring limos to collect our guests at the Portland airport on Friday and shepherd them up here."

Ivy looked from her boss to the woman who had been instrumental in getting Ivy this well-paid job. Both of them appeared oddly certain that Ivy could handle this extraordinary upcoming event. Both of them had believed in her when she was desperate and had no clue how she was going to support herself and her child.

Already, she was in their debt. What could she say other than yes?

"I'll help however I can," she said. "With one caveat."

Farrell raised an eyebrow. "And that would be?"

"I'll be the one to put Dolly to bed at night. It doesn't take long. I don't want her thinking I've abandoned her."

Katie nodded. "Of course. Besides, Quin and I will still be here that early in the evening. So no worries."

Farrell was already second-guessing himself. It was true that he needed a hostess for the weekend. But Katie had served that role in the past and would have done so again if he'd asked. Somehow, though, he believed Ivy would add an important element to the upcoming event. She was practical and adaptable. And she would tell him honestly if aspects of the summit weren't working.

Right now, she looked uneasy. Katie had thrown a lot of stuff at her, and there would be more to come. Was Farrell pushing her too far?

Before he could answer that question, Ivy stood and began clearing the table. Katie stood, as well. "I can handle cleanup," Katie said. "Ivy, the chicken salad was amazing. Farrell, you go back to work. Ivy, you put Dolly down for her nap. I've got this."

When Ivy disappeared with Dolly in her arms, Farrell shook his head slowly. "Was she open to the hostess idea?"

Katie grimaced. "Not really. I had to sell it hard. But I think you're right. She'll be an asset this weekend. And even though she had reservations about being so visible, she'll enjoy it. I hope."

After lunch, when Katie had gone down the road to her and Quin's house, Farrell went back to the lab and tried to work with little success. He wasn't worried about the summit weekend. The prospect of a new venture was exciting. But Ivy was a conundrum that stuck with him.

This past week, he'd found himself watching her when he thought she wouldn't notice. The gentle swell of her breasts. The way her hips filled out a pair of jeans. The glimmer of mischief in her eyes when she laughed.

With a mutter of disgust, he dropped his pencil and stood. All he'd managed to accomplish in the last half hour was a series of amateur doodles. He might as well take a break and satisfy his curiosity at the same time.

When he knocked on the front door of the cabin, he took a moment to appreciate how it had turned out. He had envisioned it as an addition to the three large houses he and his brothers had built here in northern Maine.

The cabin was smaller. And cozy. Maybe one day, Quin and Katie's kids would come stay in the cabin between semesters in college. Or even honeymoon here. It was a great hideaway.

He knocked a second time, and the door abruptly opened. Ivy was visibly shocked. "Farrell. Did you need me?"

Suddenly, he questioned his judgment. Ivy's face was flushed. One cheek sported a visible blanket crease. "Ah, hell," he said. "You were napping. I'm sorry. Never mind."

He turned on his heel, but Ivy's soft, unintentionally sexy voice stopped him. "You can come in, Farrell. I needed to get up anyway."

"Is the baby awake?"

"No. She'll sleep for another forty-five minutes at least."

He should have walked away. But he didn't. "I don't

want to interrupt," he said gruffly, feeling the tops of his ears get hot. There was no reason in the world for him to be here. But still, he stayed.

Ivy opened the door wider and stepped back. "You're fine. Come on in."

Together, they took the few steps to the living room. Ivy curled up in an armchair upholstered in moss green velvet. Farrell sat on the green-and-gold-plaid sofa. "Shall I start a fire?" he asked. The day was cold and dreary.

"That would be nice."

She was eyeing him with suspicion, and no wonder. He was acting weird. Even he could see that.

Conscious of her gaze on his back, he squatted beside the fireplace and put together the kindling and larger logs. With some kerosene-soaked pine cones and newspaper and a couple of matches, he soon had a creditable blaze going.

"There you go," he said, standing and brushing a bit of soot off his pants. "Is this the first one you've had?"

Ivy nodded, wrinkling her nose. "I tried twice, but apparently, pyromania is not one of my gifts."

"It takes practice," he said, sitting back down with a sigh. There were worse ways to spend a fall afternoon.

"Shouldn't you be inventing stuff?"

He chuckled. "Yes. I'm blocked at the moment. It happens."

"Am I allowed to ask what you're working on?"

"Of course. It's a motion-activated emergency signal. Sometimes in an avalanche or a climbing accident, the person involved can't use their cell phone. Maybe it's lost. Maybe the signal is poor."

"Maybe they can't reach it, or they're too badly injured to call for help?"

"Exactly. The device I'm trying to create would be triggered when there is an abrupt change in altitude. That signal could be picked up by any number of rescue frequencies."

"Impressive."

He shrugged. "It might be, if I ever get it done."

Ivy picked at a loose thread on the sofa arm. "Why did you ask me to be your hostess this weekend?"

He hadn't seen that one coming. "Well, uh…"

She pinned him with a sharp gaze. "The truth, please."

Six

Ivy couldn't believe she'd had the courage to ask the question, but she badly wanted to know.

Farrell's expression was hard to read. He shot her a glance and then stood to poke the fire. When it blazed up to his satisfaction, he leaned an arm on the mantel and faced her. "You could say my motives were multi-layered."

It was difficult to stay focused when he was such a beautiful man to look at. Despite the cerebral nature of his work, it was clear he spent a great deal of time out-doors. The honey streaks in his brown hair were natural. His skin was tanned to a golden color, and his sinewy muscles were that of an experienced athlete.

She had studied up on the Stone brothers. Google was a wonderful thing. Quin, Katie's husband, had missed a gold medal for skiing by a fraction of a second. She'd seen photos of a laughing Zachary camel racing in Morocco. And as for Farrell, well, he seemed to have been everywhere and done everything. Maybe grief had made it too hard to stay in Maine, or maybe he simply liked the challenge of climbing mountains and flying over glaciers.

"Multilayered," she muttered. "That's not an answer."

"Fine," he said, sounding grumpy. "I thought it would be fun for you."

"Wait, what?" As the words penetrated her fog, she frowned. "Since when do I need to have fun?"

"*Everybody* needs to have fun, Ivy. And I've been told that new moms sometimes struggle, because they get overwhelmed with the demands of a baby, and they begin to miss adult interactions."

"I don't want you *handling* me," Ivy said defensively. "I'm perfectly capable of looking after myself."

His green eyes sparked with irritation. "Of course you are. But I also thought you might be an asset this weekend, because you aren't part of Stone River Outdoors. I was hoping you could give us a new perspective. We want to do more of these co-op weekends. You can comment on things that Zachary and Quin and Katie and I might not see, because we're too close to the subject matter. I'd like to hear what you think when it's all over."

Shame was not a good feeling. "Oh," she said stiffly. "Well, that's different. I'm sure I'll enjoy it."

Her prim assurance made him grin. "No, you're not.

But you're also probably a little bit curious. So you agreed."

"I agreed because you're my boss."

His face went blank. "I see." He stood abruptly and headed for the door. "Then forget about it. Katie will handle what needs to be done. I'm sorry to intrude."

Now she had really done it. "Wait," she cried. She ran after him and caught him at the door. When she put her hand on his forearm, all the air left her lungs. Until Farrell entered her life, she hadn't touched a man who wasn't her husband in over a decade. From what she remembered of the opposite sex, those long-ago college boys hadn't felt like this.

Farrell's arm was muscled, warm, strong enough to rescue a woman if she needed rescuing. "I'm sorry," she said urgently, making herself step back. "You're right. I *was* curious, and even though I'm scared, I'm honored that you offered me this opportunity."

"I don't want your gratitude," he snapped. He ran a hand over his face and leaned back against the door. "I don't understand you, Ivy, but I'm trying. I'm not the enemy here."

"No," she said. "You're not."

"Do you want to talk about it?" His green-eyed gaze, clear and steady, told her he had pieced together at least some of her truth. On his face, she saw compassion. Kindness. Wariness.

She wanted to… She desperately wanted to tell him everything that had happened to her. But she was so ashamed. "No," she said. "Not today. Maybe never. But it's kind of you to ask."

"I'll tell you about Sasha," he said abruptly. "If you ever want to know. Not a quid pro quo. My tragedy is further in the past than yours. I don't expect you to bare your soul to me."

Tragedy wasn't the right word, but she couldn't explain. "Now," she said quietly. "Tell me about Sasha now. If you have time."

Some of the tension in his shoulders relaxed. "I don't talk about her often. But you're someone who would understand."

"Then sit down," Ivy said. "I'll behave."

He touched her cheek with a single fingertip, barely a brushstroke, the flutter of a butterfly wing. "Don't make promises you can't keep."

They had reached some kind of milestone, Ivy realized. She had let down her guard, and Farrell, without her noticing, had slipped into her heart and made a place for himself.

"So how did you meet?" she asked, when they resumed their seats. The fire burned merrily. The room was warm. She saw the giant inhalation and exhalation that lifted his chest and let it fall.

Perhaps to him, the tragedy didn't seem so long ago after all.

"High school," Farrell said simply. "Once we realized it was more than puppy love, we knew it was forever. But my father intervened. Sasha's background wasn't as privileged as mine. He sent me to school on the West Coast, and he manipulated Sasha's emotions."

"What did you do?"

"We waited for each other," he said simply. "I graduated. We were both twenty-one by then. There was nothing more for my father to destroy. Eventually, she won him over. We had three wonderful years. I look back sometimes and ask myself if they were really as good as I remember."

"But they were."

He nodded slowly, his gaze focused on something far away. "They were incredible. Right up until the day she was diagnosed with a rare, aggressive form of breast cancer. She made it eleven months and died holding my hand."

"I'm so sorry, Farrell." The idea that he had found such a beautiful love and lost it broke her heart.

He shook his head as if to remove the threads that bound him to the past. "You understand what it's like. I don't know if your husband's death was unexpected or if, like me, you had time to say goodbye. Either way, death sucks. That door slams shut, and no matter how much you try to pry it open, the person on the other side is gone."

Ivy found herself in a quandary. She could let his assumptions ride. But he was being so wonderfully decent and open and amazingly kind, her lies by omission choked her.

"I do understand. In a way. But my experience was not like yours."

He grimaced. "Death never is…"

"You lost the great love of your life."

"Yes. I did."

She stared down at her lap, unable to face him. "I didn't," she whispered. "I'm not grieving like you have all these years."

* * *

Farrell tried to conceal his shock. What was she saying? Talking about Sasha had not been as painful as he'd expected. Particularly with someone who had been through a similar experience. Since Ivy was recently widowed, he'd wanted to encourage her to open up about her loss. Apparently, he was way off base. Now he was speechless.

Though as he sifted through what he knew of Ivy, hadn't he guessed there might have been something amiss?

He cleared his throat. "I see."

"No," she said. "You don't. And I can't explain. But I'm so glad you had someone like Sasha in your life. No matter what happens down the road, no one can take that away from you."

"I would never betray your confidence," he said slowly. "It's not healthy to keep things bottled inside."

Her smile was gently mocking. "Psychology 101?"

He thought about it for a moment. "No. Actually, personal experience. I had to see a counselor after Sasha died. I couldn't deal with the emotions. I'd been brought up to believe that men don't whine and they sure as hell don't cry. But I was on the verge of a breakdown, I think. It was Zachary who finally made me go. I owe him a lot. He and Quin, both."

Suddenly, Dolly's plaintive cries came through on the monitor. Farrell lurched to his feet, wildly relieved to have an escape route. What in the hell had he started?

"She's awake," he said. "I should get back to the lab. I'll let myself out."

For the remainder of the afternoon, he worked on his project with half of his brain. But the gray matter that was unoccupied kept poking at the Ivy situation.

She isn't grieving? He knew a bit about denial. All the stages of grief, in fact, were familiar to him. He'd experienced every one of them in varying degrees.

Was Ivy still in shock? Was that it? She'd said in her interview that her husband had died *a few months ago.* That could mean three or six or nine. When Farrell had asked if the baby's dad had time to know his daughter, Ivy had shut down that conversation quickly.

Fortunately, Katie and Quin were coming over for dinner tonight. If not, Farrell would have been hard-pressed to know what to say to Ivy when he saw her again.

As it was, the evening unfolded naturally. Ivy prepared an incredible meal of beef Stroganoff, spinach salad and homemade bread. Dolly played happily with metal spoons in her high chair while the adults chatted.

Quin seemed particularly taken with the baby. "She's really sweet and smart," he said.

Ivy laughed. "And now you're my new best friend. Praising a woman's child is a sure way to win points."

"But it's true," Quin protested. "Has she started walking yet?"

"No. It's not quite time. Possibly in eight or ten weeks. Or later—who knows? I've heard everything from eight months to fifteen months."

Katie helped Ivy dish up the apple pie and ice cream

for dessert. "Quin was always ahead of the curve physically. Or so I've heard."

Farrell snorted. "Did he tell you that? I'd take my baby brother's boasts with a grain of salt. He once broke his wrist falling out of bed. Quin wasn't exactly a child prodigy when it came to athletics."

While Quin and Katie squabbled good-naturedly about his childhood exploits, Farrell glanced over at Ivy and caught her watching the other two with a smile on her face.

He was stunned. Why had he ever thought she was not conventionally beautiful? Her face lit up with humor and amusement. The smile altered her serious expression, gave life and energy to her delicate features.

The unexpected transformation left him breathless. He was drawn to her…to Ivy, this complex woman with the prickly exterior. Telling her about Sasha had fulfilled a need he didn't know he had. Other people always wanted to "make it better." Ivy simply listened.

As Katie and Quin continued their pretend argument, Ivy joined in, her sharp wit and dry remarks egging them on. Farrell understood suddenly that he was seeing the real woman behind the careful mask.

That very first day in his Portland office, he'd met a fragile female beaten down by life. A person who had hit bottom. A new mother, lost and afraid.

Katie must have seen it, too, and Katie being Katie, she had decided Ivy needed to be Farrell's new hire. Not for Farrell's sake, but for Ivy's.

Who or what had turned Ivy Danby from the glow-ing, confident girl he suspected she once had been into a frightened shadow of herself?

He had a suspicion or two. Both of which made him sick to his stomach. But before he jumped to any conclusions, he would have to get Ivy to trust him. She was growing more comfortable day by day. There was time.

But what was he going to do about the other? The reluctant attraction? He suspected it went both ways, but he couldn't be sure. And even if he *was* sure, Ivy was too vulnerable right now.

Eventually, the others noticed that he wasn't joining in the fun.

Quin gestured theatrically. "Jeez, even my own brother isn't jumping in to defend me. Tell her, Farrell. Tell Ivy how good I was at everything in junior high and high school."

"Well," Farrell drawled. "There was that D+ you made in chemistry. And the C- in calculus. Is that what you mean?"

Ivy and Katie giggled when Quin glared. "Sports," he said between clenched teeth. "Tell her how good I was at sports."

"Oh." Farrell smiled at Ivy. "My brother was good at sports."

The smile she gave him was utterly sweet and uncomplicated. It packed a powerful punch. "So I've heard," she said.

Perhaps kindly, she changed the subject. "What about Zachary?" she asked. "The two of you are the first and the last. How does Zachary fit into your family dynamics?"

There was a split second of silence while Quin looked at Farrell and vice versa. Quin rubbed his chin, grinning. "Zachary is what one might call a ladies' man."

Katie shook her head. "Oh, please. Don't be ridiculous. Zachary is wonderful, Ivy," she said. "Don't let them lead you astray. Zachary is a perfect gentleman. It's true that he dates a lot, but that's not a crime."

Quin stood up to pour more wine. "The phrase *girl in every port* comes to mind."

Ivy accepted the refill with a smile. "And will he have a lady friend in tow when he arrives?"

"Not this time," Katie said. "Next weekend is going to be an important business function. Most of my brother-in-law's girlfriends can't even spell *business*."

Farrell chuckled. "Now who's being catty?"

Katie looked guilty. "I shouldn't have said that. You'll like him, Ivy. He's a sweetheart."

Quin nodded. "Who knows—maybe he'll take a shine to Ivy. It would do him good to meet a woman of substance."

Farrell tensed. Incredibly, jealousy curled in his gut. "Ivy is recently widowed. This conversation is in poor taste."

The room fell silent. Ivy was visibly mortified. She glared at him. "They were just having a bit of fun." She turned to the other two. "I enjoyed dinner. If you'll excuse me, I need to take Dolly to the cabin and get her ready for bed."

Katie protested. "Oh, don't go yet. Can't you put her down in the port-a-crib? And carry her to the cabin later? I'll help."

Ivy hesitated.

Quin gave her a hangdog expression. "Sorry, Miss Ivy. I won't do it again, I swear."

Farrell had reached his limit in a lot of ways. "I'm sure Ivy is tired. It's been a long day." Only after the words left his mouth did he realize how he sounded. As if he was glad to be rid of her.

Ivy's face turned red. Katie shot him a bewildered glance. She patted Ivy's arm. "I'll come with you to the cabin for some girl talk. You don't mind, do you?" She scooped Dolly out of her high chair. "Besides, I can't get enough of this sweetie pie."

When the women walked out of the house, Quin stared at Farrell. "What the hell is wrong with you, man?"

Farrell rubbed his temples where a headache was beginning to pound. "I don't know. Nothing, really. Let's forget about it."

"You acted like a jackass. Embarrassed Ivy on the one hand, and then practically shoved her out of the house. That kind of wacko behavior is bad for employee retention, you know."

"Enough, Quin," he snapped. "Just because you're nauseatingly happy doesn't mean the rest of us are."

His brother's eyes widened, then filled with sympathy. "Damn, Farrell. It's been so long since you were interested in a woman, I didn't see the signs. That's it. Am I right? You've got the hots for sweet little Ivy Danby, and it's making you crazy." Quin shook his head slowly. "As someone who only recently was on the precipice of romantic disaster myself, I feel your pain."

"I'm not interested in Ivy Danby," Farrell protested. But the words lacked heat.

Quin sobered. "Maybe you shouldn't go there, bro. You, of all people, know how long it takes to deal with grief. The timing is off. You'll only hurt yourself. Or maybe her."

"Do you think I don't know that?" Farrell muttered.

"I've never known you to do something rash. You're our rock-steady big brother. I can't handle a ripple in the force."

Farrell grinned weakly. "You are so full of it. I guess that must be what regular sex does for a guy."

Quin leaned his chair back on two legs and laced his hands across his flat belly. "Marriage is the best institution in the world. I can't believe I waited so long to try it."

Seven

Ivy was humiliated and hurt by Farrell's behavior during the impromptu Friday night dinner party. She couldn't decide if she was happy or sad that Katie and Quin headed back to Portland Saturday morning.

Their presence meant that Ivy didn't have to speak directly to Farrell. But with them gone, it was easier to simply avoid her boss.

When he had talked to her about Sasha, she felt a moment of *something*. A simple connection born of shared experiences? But if there had been a fleeting second of kinship, it was gone.

Perhaps he regretted being so honest with Ivy. Men didn't usually spill their guts with ease. He had said there was no expectation of reciprocity, but deep down she suspected that wasn't true.

Farrell was curious about Ivy. About her past.

She liked him. A lot. But not enough to dredge up the worst of her secrets. Farrell's tale about a man and a woman who were high school sweethearts—and then one of them died—was a tender, innocent story of loss.

Ivy couldn't begin to compete.

For the remainder of the weekend and the days that followed, she worked hard getting Farrell's house in order. It wasn't a huge chore. Everything had been pretty much shipshape when she arrived. But there was always the occasional dust bunny to corral and rugs to be vacuumed.

She had his breakfast waiting every morning. His lunch prepared. And a decent dinner in the evenings. What she did *not* do was eat with him anymore. She offered up excuses, and he accepted them at face value.

Whenever he returned to the main house, his handsome face was sculpted in planes and angles. No emerald-eyed smiles. No teasing remarks. They had somehow ended up on opposite sides of an enormous chasm.

Dolly, thank goodness, was happy almost all the time. She was such an easy baby. Ivy knew how lucky she was. This job would be much more difficult with a cranky infant to juggle.

As promised by Katie, several boxes landed on Farrell's doorstep, all of them addressed to Ivy. During naptime for the next few days, Ivy tried on her new wardrobe.

Katie might have grown up in a modest household, but her instincts for fashion were spot-on. As much as Ivy had dreaded this Pygmalion-like makeover, it turned out to be not so bad. None of her new clothes made her feel self-conscious. In fact, they boosted her self-esteem considerably.

It had been years since she'd had anything new to wear. Now the pile of dresses and pants and shoes and jewelry—and even underwear—on the guest bed made her dizzy with anticipation.

Despite their current differences, she wanted to make Farrell proud. He had invested a great deal of time and money in this upcoming house party. She would do her part.

Tuesday morning, Ivy received a text from Katie. The chef was bringing everything with her, but she had asked if there were several large platters available. Ivy promised to check.

As was her custom now, Ivy put Dolly down around ten in the port-a-crib in Farrell's beautiful study. The walls were lined with floor-to-ceiling bookshelves. Several of the paintings looked wildly expensive, though Ivy was no art critic. She closed the heavy velvet drapes and turned on a tiny fan that would provide enough white noise for Dolly to sleep peacefully.

With the baby monitor in hand, Ivy tiptoed out of the room and closed the door. She remembered seeing serving pieces in one of the cabinets. Once she located them, she would text Katie what was available.

Farrell's home had ten-foot ceilings, which made the kitchen beautiful and roomy. But it also meant that the highest of the cabinet shelves were far above Ivy's reach. As a "vertically challenged" adult, she had spent her life on her tiptoes or asking for help.

But Farrell was tucked away in the lab, and she didn't

want to bother him, certainly not after what had happened Friday. They had barely exchanged a dozen words in the interim. He was gruff and monotone. She was equally withdrawn. They had achieved an uneasy détente.

In the pantry, she found a small two-step stool. It wasn't much, but it might work. She moved around the room, examining each cabinet. Finally, she found what she had remembered spotting on an earlier scouting mission.

Stacked one on top of each other were three stoneware platters, clearly handmade. The graduated sizes would probably work for whatever the chef had in mind. The free-form swirls of gray and navy and green were elegant and well suited to the ambience in Farrell's beautiful home.

Ivy could only touch the edge of the bottom tray. And pottery was notoriously heavy. The last thing she needed was to break them.

With her hands on her hips, she debated her options. A return to the pantry produced no answers until she spotted an old phone book on a bottom shelf. She made a mental note to recycle it, but in the meantime, the thick paper publication might be just the thing.

Carefully, she adjusted the stool. Then she rested the phone book in the exact center. Holding on to two cabinet handles to steady herself, she stepped up onto her new perch. Bingo. Now she could get her hands on the top piece of pottery. If she slid it off the pile carefully, she could step down, set it aside and go back for the other two.

* * *

Farrell was restless. And his coffee had run dry. The project was going well despite the turmoil in his gut. He'd managed to separate the two portions of his life for a few hours, but now the prospect that he might run into Ivy drew him back to the main house.

When he entered quietly and rounded the corner into the kitchen, his chest squeezed. Tiny, five-foot-three Ivy Danby was perched precariously on what looked like a damn phone book, about to break her neck.

He roared at her, his heart in his throat. "What in the hell are you doing? Are you crazy?" He lunged across the room at her, desperate to break her fall. And she was surely going to fall. The heavy platter above her head already teetered.

When he jumped in front of her and reached for the stoneware, Ivy flinched backward and threw her hands in front of her face.

He was so shocked, he barely caught her before she lost her balance. If he had left well enough alone, she might have managed her balancing act, but it was too late. The platter eluded both of them and shattered on the floor.

Farrell felt a piece hit his ankle, but he was more worried about Ivy. She was glassy-eyed with shock. And she avoided his gaze.

Without speaking another word, he scooped up the monitor and carried Ivy across the hall into his bedroom. It was the closest place that had a sofa. The master suite was huge and included a seating area. He set her down and crouched in front of her. "Ivy," he said, the next words stuck in his throat. He was still trying to process them. "Did you think I was going to hit you?"

She was pale as milk, big-eyed, tragic. "Yes," she whispered.

If she had struck him, the shock would have been less. He sat back on his ass, horrified. Aghast. Suddenly, so many things made sense.

His mouth was dry. His brain spun in a million directions.

Those hazel eyes filled with tears. Eventually, drops spilled over and ran down her cheeks. The fact that Ivy's distress was completely silent made it worse somehow.

Though he was afraid of upsetting her further, he couldn't bear to see her like this. Carefully, he stood and joined her on the sofa, putting his arm around her shoulders and trying to convey his compassion and concern.

If she had evaded his touch or seemed uncomfortable in any way, he would have released her immediately. But Ivy turned into his embrace and buried her face against his shoulder. The quiet tears turned into sobs that shook her small frame.

One of her hands gripped his shirt as if she were trying to latch on to something in the midst of a storm. Her fingers clenched the cloth right over his heart.

He held her loosely, his throat painful with emotions he didn't try to analyze. It was clear to him now how very badly he wanted her. Her feminine curves made him ache. The sexual hunger was something he couldn't control. But he didn't have to let her know. And he sure as hell didn't have to let himself get sucked into this relationship that was bound to tear him apart.

It already was, though he had tried to keep his distance.

Eventually, the tears ran out. He suspected they had been building for a very long time. He suddenly realized that he was stroking her hair. That had to stop.

Ivy exhaled on a shuddering breath. "I'm sorry," she muttered. When she tried to stand up, he released her immediately. "I should check on the baby," she said.

Farrell pointed to the tiny screen on the monitor. "She hasn't stirred. Talk to me, Ivy. Or if not me, someone. Katie, maybe?"

Ivy wiped the tears from her face with her hands and then wrapped her arms around her waist. She chewed her bottom lip. "It's not exactly what you think."

"So your husband didn't physically abuse you?" He heard the angry indignation in his voice. Ivy did also.

When she spoke again, there was almost no emotion on her face. "This is a long story," she warned.

Farrell realized in that instant that he had a choice. He could make an excuse and go back to the lab. Ivy would let him leave without protest. Maybe she might even be glad. The two of them would continue in a guarded employer/employee relationship.

His other option was to try helping her. And thus open himself up to a deeper relationship. One that on his side, at least, had the potential to develop into something more.

He had run from intimacy for seven years. His life

was on an even keel now. No devastating lows. But no exhilarating highs either.

Did he really want to let Ivy into his heart? She had already carved out a tiny niche in his life. Could he handle anything more?

He cleared his throat. "I'm listening, Ivy. And I'm not going anywhere."

For a moment, tears threatened again. He watched as she blinked them back. Twisted her hands. Composed herself.

"Richard was ten years older than me," she said quietly. "A professor at my college. In the business department. I didn't have any classes with him, but we had met a time or two. When my parents were killed in a boating accident during the final semester of my senior year, it was Richard who kept tabs on my assignments and made sure I graduated."

"Why would he do that?"

She shrugged. "I thought at the time he was simply a nice person. I was drowning in grief. As an only child, I was utterly bereft. Richard made himself indispensable."

"And then what happened?"

"I've had some counseling in recent years," she said. "And read some books on the subject. I understand now that he used my vulnerability to groom me. It was all very gradual and unremarkable. I didn't even realize that he was carefully separating me from the few relatives who could have provided a link to my parents. It was the same with my classmates. If I thought about it, I concluded that my girlfriends and I had all drifted apart after graduation. Soon, Richard was the only constant in my world."

"He was a predator," Farrell said flatly, trying to keep his anger under control. Ivy didn't need that from him.

Her bottom lip trembled, but she didn't agree or disagree with him. "There were dinners and long conversations in his office," she said. "One day he kissed me. Four months after graduation, we were married."

"And then he started hitting you?" Farrell was incensed on her behalf, but Ivy actually smiled. It was a heartbreaking smile, but it was a smile. "Richard's thing was control. He was obsessive about everything in his environment. Forget arguing about which way the toilet paper should unroll from the dispenser. Richard wanted the cabinets and the refrigerator organized daily. He expected me to accommodate his every whim. And I did," she said simply. "Because he had done so much for me."

"When did you first know something was wrong?"

"Two years after my parents died, their loss finally became manageable. It was like coming out of a fog for me. People say that grief is different for everyone, and that's true. When I started thinking about the future, I realized I was healing. I knew it was time to get a job."

"What was your major?"

"Early childhood education. I filled out applications and began interviewing with principals for positions in the fall. I didn't tell Richard, because I wanted to surprise him."

"Did you get hired?"

"I had callbacks for some follow-up interviews, but

before that could happen, Richard found out. He was furious. Not simply irritated that I had initiated this step without consulting him, but completely berserk with rage. At first, I was confused. But when I had the temerity to defend myself, he backhanded me so hard I slammed into the wall."

"My God, Ivy." Farrell didn't know what to say. He felt ill.

"It only happened that one time. He apologized instantly. But he insisted that our family life would run more smoothly if I stayed at home. He said he made plenty of money for the two of us to live comfortably."

"As a college professor?"

"He had a second job. In fact, he traveled often for two and three days at a time. I wondered how his class load worked with his schedule, but I didn't ask. I learned early on that he didn't like explaining himself."

Farrell frowned. "So you didn't teach?"

"No. I convinced myself that I was overreacting. Of *course* he was hurt that I would hunt for a job without telling him. And I knew that some men were supermacho and liked supporting their wives. It wasn't the life I had planned for myself, but I told myself that all couples compromise."

"Only Richard wasn't compromising," Farrell said, wishing the guy was alive so he could beat the hell out of him.

Ivy sat suddenly in the chair opposite the sofa, as if her legs would no longer support her. She stared down at her hands for long seconds. Farrell knew better than to offer his analysis. This might be the only time Ivy would open up to him. If he inserted himself too much into her story, she would stop talking.

She seemed so small and fragile to him. He could only imagine what she had endured. A woman had to be very strong to come out of that situation and still be able to function.

"I've been so ashamed and embarrassed," she said, the words little more than a whisper.

He leaned forward, staring at her intently. "Why, Ivy? You're not to blame for anything."

Now she faced him bravely, her heart-shaped face, pointed chin and short haircut making her seem younger than her thirty-two years. "I didn't leave him," she said, her voice breaking. "I let three years go by. Then five, then six. He tracked my phone. He doled out my *allowance*. Because I wasn't allowed to get a job, I sneaked around and baked cakes and pies for the neighbors and squirreled away that money in a secret spot in the house."

"Because you knew you were going to leave eventually?"

"Maybe. Subconsciously. But first, I used it to see a counselor. With her help, I finally understood that the gratitude I felt he deserved for saving me after my parents died was a false equivalency. His original kindness was a means of subjugating me, so I didn't owe him anything."

"That must have been a bitter pill to swallow."

She nodded, her expression revealing relief. "I wasn't sure you would be able to understand. I felt so stupid and clueless. I'd let a borderline psychopath take over my life. During a year and a half of therapy I gradually saw the truth of what had happened to me. Harder still was learning to forgive myself."

"And then?"

"I told the therapist I wanted to leave him. She was concerned about my physical safety. I told her he had only hit me that one time. Still, he was clearly capable of violence."

Farrell knew there was worse to come. His stomach recoiled, but he kept his expression calm. "So did you leave or not?"

"He must have suspected. I did everything I could to act *normal*. But one night when he came home from a trip, he…" She stopped, swallowed hard and gave Farrell a look that hurt him to his core. "You don't need the details. But he sabotaged my birth control."

Eight

"Ivy..."

Farrell's look of compassion made her determined to show him she had survived. And thrived. "It was bad, but it convinced me the marriage was over."

"And then you left him?"

She shook her head, remembering the anguish she had felt. "I found out I was pregnant."

Before Farrell could respond to that, she glanced at the monitor in relief. "Dolly is awake," she said. "I should go get her."

She fled. There was no other word for it. In the study, she scooped up her perfect daughter and hugged her so tightly the baby protested.

"Sorry, love," Ivy said. Tears threatened, but no. She. Would. Not. Cry. Not now. The worst was over. Telling

Farrell her story, or at least most of it, left her feeling like that awful dream where you're standing outside naked and you can't find your way home.

She was raw and exhausted but oddly calm.

Though it was cowardly, she sneaked out the side door of the house and made a beeline for the safety of her cabin. *Her* cabin. Already, it seemed like home. How long would Farrell want to work up here near the Canadian border? Two months? Three? What would Ivy do when he no longer needed her?

The baby's routine normalized the afternoon. Dolly had been crawling for some time now, but today, she was brave enough to reach for the edge of the sofa and pull up onto one knee.

"Careful, little munchkin. Don't get ahead of yourself." Would Dolly be walking by Christmas?

Thinking of the holidays was a mistake. Surely Farrell would go back to Portland for Christmas. Would he allow his housekeeper and her daughter to stay behind?

Ivy desperately wanted permanence for her child. Traditions. Continuity. The thought of staying here in the Maine woods during the winter was delightful. But without Farrell, everything would seem flat. Ivy had come to depend on his gentle good humor, his deep laugh, the sexy way his eyes crinkled when he smiled.

She cared about him.

While Dolly took her afternoon nap, Ivy made a batch of chocolate-chip cookies. She would take them to Farrell as a peace offering. Or a thank-you. Not many people wanted to hear what Ivy's life had been like. Fewer still offered to listen.

Farrell's presence as a quiet, compassionate sounding board had been cathartic. Though Ivy was desperately attracted to him, she wondered if the feeling was one-sided. There were moments when she thought *something* hovered between them. But that might be her overactive imagination.

It was mortifying to remember how she had shrunk away from him when he tried to keep her from falling. Some atavistic instinct for survival had brought back old coping mechanisms.

She hadn't told Farrell the whole truth. Perhaps it wasn't important now.

Suddenly, she remembered the broken platter in the kitchen. She should have cleaned up that mess already. And now it was time to begin dinner.

After packaging the still-warm cookies, Ivy collected the baby and set out for the big house. When she entered the kitchen, it was spotless. Not a sign of broken pottery anywhere. The remaining platters sat out on the counter. Ivy paused long enough to text Katie the required information.

Then she set the cookies on the island and went in search of her boss. She wasn't a coward. She hadn't done anything wrong.

She found Farrell on the front porch replacing a section of the railing. He looked up when she stepped out of the house. Something pulsed between them. Awareness. Awkwardness. "I brought fresh cookies," she said, adjusting Dolly on her hip. "If you're hungry."

He stood and stretched. Ivy watched him, unable to look away. He was perfect. Tall. Strong. Intelligent. The muscles in his arms and shoulders were visible through his gray knit shirt.

The bottom fell out of her stomach, and her knees went shaky. She was more than attracted to him. She *wanted* him. The knowledge troubled her. Farrell Stone was the last man on earth she should set her sights on.

Farrell had lost so much, faced such devastating sadness. Ivy's emotional baggage was probably daunting for a man like him.

In the kitchen, they shared cookies and milk, their hands occasionally brushing as they passed a plate or reached for seconds. Ivy wondered if Farrell experienced the same sense of intimacy she did. Unfortunately, the vignette was *too* intimate, too perfect for Ivy's peace of mind.

To break the mood, she made herself open the pantry and peruse the choices for dinner.

Farrell spoke from behind her shoulder. "Forget fixing dinner," he said.

When she turned, puzzled, she caught him sneaking a fourth cookie, his expression guilt-ridden.

"A grown man can't live on sugar," she said as he licked chocolate from his fingertips. The way he was enjoying her baked offering pleased her.

"Not true," he said, grinning.

Her stomach quivered. Suddenly, she could see Farrell in bed with a woman, kissing his way from her belly to her—

Dear Lord... She slammed the pantry door and cleared her throat. "Well, I can't. What did you have in mind?"

"I ordered pizza," he said calmly.

"You're kidding me. Aren't we twenty miles from the nearest town with a pizza joint?"

"More like twenty-five. But it's amazing how the promise of a hundred-dollar tip motivates people."

"You didn't have to do that," she muttered, knowing he was thinking of her. "I could have fixed dinner."

He brushed the back of his hand over her hot cheek and took Dolly from her. "We could all use a junkfood night. It will be fun. And nothing to clean up. Am I right?"

His smile, though it wasn't at all suggestive, made her heart beat faster. "Pizza does sound good."

"I ordered three different kinds. Wasn't sure what you would like."

"Farrell…" She blurted out his name.

He glanced at her and froze. "What is it, Ivy?"

Her face must have revealed her agitation. "You don't have to feel sorry for me," she said bluntly. "In fact, I don't want you to. I'm fine."

His narrow gaze made those green-and-gold irises burn bright. It was his turn to hesitate. But afterward, his jaw firmed as if he had decided that too much tiptoeing around the elephant in the room was a bad idea.

"Here's the thing, Ivy," he said. "Your emotionally fragile state is the only thing keeping me from kissing you, so I think it's best if I *do* feel sorry for you. At least for now. It's safer that way."

She gaped at him, her cheeks going hot. "You want to kiss me?"

"Yes," he said, tickling her daughter's tummy. "I do."

* * *

Farrell would have laughed at Ivy's startled expression had the situation been different. She stood frozen, trying to process what he had said. He could almost see the wheels turning in her head.

When she didn't come up with an answer, he leaned against the cabinet and put Dolly on his shoulders, letting her play with his hair. "Have I shocked you?" he asked.

"Um… I…" Still, Ivy stuttered.

"Why is that so hard to believe?"

"I'm not beautiful. Men like you and your brothers go out with beautiful women. It's a billionaire rule."

Her wry silliness amused him. "You *are* beautiful," he said. "Not in a runway-model way, perhaps. But you're something even better. You have an interesting face. A body that's so sexy it keeps me up at night, and a smile, although infrequent, that lights up a room. I find you utterly charming, Ivy Danby, and I'm not sure what to do about that."

The front doorbell rang, saving Ivy from having to respond. Farrell pulled a wad of cash out of his pocket. "Dolly and I will grab the pizza. Why don't you set the table?"

When he returned, balancing a squirmy baby and two very warm cardboard boxes, Ivy couldn't quite meet his eyes.

"Here," she said. "Let me take her."

In the handoff, Farrell's hand brushed the side of her chest. It wasn't deliberate. Even so, feeling the soft weight of her breast made him suck in a shocked breath.

Maybe he'd been attracted to her since that first day. Was it because she needed *saving*, and he liked being a hero? Or was the pull something more visceral?

They ate mostly in silence, except for Dolly, who jabbered constantly. The baby was a convenient third party, a place to center his attention. Ivy followed his example.

Why had he told Ivy he wanted to kiss her? Now that he'd said it, kissing her was all he could think about.

She was wearing her old clothes—soft faded jeans and a fleecy pullover in cinnamon. The color flattered her, made her skin glow. "Have another piece of pizza," he said. Ivy had eaten three to his six.

"No, thanks. I'm stuffed."

He combined the remaining slices into one box and put them in the fridge. Then he returned to the table, sat down and stared at her. "May I ask you something?"

Alarm flashed across her face. "Yes."

"Will you put the baby to sleep here? In the study? You and I didn't finish our conversation earlier. I'd like to hear the rest of your story."

"It's not important," she muttered. Her face had gone pale, her hazel-eyed gaze momentarily haunted.

If that had been the truth, perhaps he would have let it go. But he suspected Ivy needed to get the poison out of her system. Deprive her memories of their power.

He knew something about that process. Years ago, when he was finally able to let himself think of Sasha and not exert all his energy pretending those memories didn't exist, the healing had begun.

Ivy had suffered. She was still suffering. Maybe it

wasn't his place to help her. But he was the only one around.

"Please," he said.

The silent standoff lasted for a minute or more as Ivy looked anywhere but at him. With a sigh, she stood and nodded. "I'll have to grab her pajamas and a couple other things."

"No problem. This little lady and I will entertain ourselves until you get back."

When Ivy left the kitchen, Farrell scooped the baby out of her high chair and carried her into his bedroom. "How would you like to play with a brand-new toothbrush?"

Ivy scurried around in the cabin, picking up everything she would need for Dolly's bedtime routine. Farrell didn't have a rocking chair, but Ivy could walk the floor and sing to her. That always worked.

She was only gone twenty-five minutes. When she returned, Farrell's kitchen was empty. She followed the sound of his voice and found her boss and her daughter on Farrell's giant king-size bed. Dolly was playing with a…toothbrush?

"Not to worry," Farrell said quickly. "It's fresh out of the wrapper."

The scene should have looked domestic. But it didn't, not entirely. Farrell *wasn't* the baby's daddy enjoying time at the end of the day with his offspring. Instead, he resembled a dangerous, lazy jungle cat sprawled on his side. A lock of hair tumbled across his forehead.

Dolly had probably pulled on it. Hair torture was one of her favorite games.

Ivy stopped several paces from the bed. It was a huge four-poster. But not traditional. The wood was light, the design probably Amish or Shaker. The solid navy bedspread looked wildly expensive. She didn't get out much, but she had perused a lot of catalogs over the years. The only difference was, Farrell's bed didn't have a dozen fancy pillows. He wasn't the type to go for that kind of stuff.

Even without an allotment of extra shams and bolsters, everything in this master suite screamed wealth and sophistication. When she cleaned his bathroom each week, she was struck by the fact that it offered every possible luxurious amenity. From heated floors and heated towel racks to the hedonistic shower, this was a rich man's world.

She cleared her throat. "I'll take her now."

Farrell smiled. "If you must. She has a lot of personality for such a little person."

Ivy managed to snag Dolly without getting too close to the jungle cat. "She really does. Some days I wish she wouldn't grow up so fast."

"Why don't you meet me in the living room when you're done?"

It was phrased politely, but he had asked her to finish her life story, and Ivy had agreed. Why had she said yes?

As she changed Dolly into her pajamas and sang to her, Ivy found herself unsettled. This familiar nighttime routine was as much for mother as daughter. Tonight, there was no calm to be had.

When Dolly was asleep, Ivy tiptoed out of the study and stopped by the hall bathroom to freshen up. She could have changed into one of her new outfits, but those were for the house party. And besides, she didn't want Farrell to think she was primping for him.

She still didn't believe he wanted to kiss her. He'd probably said that to bolster her self-esteem. It was kind of him, but not very believable. She would bet a lot of money that he was still in love with his dead wife.

When she finally made her way into the living room, it was completely dark outside. A front had moved through in the last hour, bringing a drizzling rain and dropping temps into the low sixties. Farrell had built a fire that crackled and popped with warmth and cheer.

The overhead lights were off, but several lamps burned around the room. He had pulled two armchairs in front of the blaze. A bottle of wine and two glasses sat on the small table in between.

Farrell looked up when she entered the room. "Is she asleep?"

"Completely. I know how lucky I am that she's an easy baby."

"True. We have employees at Stone River Outdoors who come back from maternity leave or family leave looking haggard. No sleep for nights on end. It must be rough."

Ivy sat down in one of the plush, comfy armchairs and sighed. She kicked off her shoes and curled her legs beneath her. "I know. Particularly if you're the kind of person who needs a full eight hours."

Farrell laughed and joined her by the fire. "I'd say we all *need* it, but very few people I know manage to make it happen."

"May I ask you a personal question?" she said.

Something flickered across his face, but he nodded. "Sure."

"Why did you build such a big house for just you? I know you entertain, but was that the only reason?"

Farrell stared at the fire, his jaw carved in stone. She saw his shoulders lift and fall, and he scooted deeper into his chair. "Sasha wanted it," he said, the words barely audible. "We planned to have lots of kids. She was a good amateur artist. One day when she was sick, she drew this exact house. Then made a joke. Said if she didn't make it, I should build the house anyway."

"She wasn't serious?"

"No. It was only a way for her to entertain herself when days were bad. But it was always only the outside of the house she drew. She said a view of the ocean like this one deserved a worthy house on the cliff. After she died, I built it. Closure, I guess." He shrugged. "I like to think she knows."

Ivy's throat tightened, and tears stung her eyes. She couldn't imagine being loved like that. "I'm sorry if my question made you sad," she croaked. "I was curious."

"I'm fine. It was a long time ago."

Nine

The silence between them now was awkward. Farrell blamed himself. Why did he have to bring Sasha into the conversation? Ivy never would have known the difference. All Farrell had to say was that he wanted a large space for entertaining.

Maybe he was summoning Sasha's ghost to prevent himself from doing something stupid.

"Would you like wine?" He blurted it out, feeling alarmingly off-balance. With the chilly weather and the cozy setup he had created, this suddenly looked like more than it was.

"Yes," Ivy said.

He uncorked the bottle of Syrah and poured two glasses. "Cheers," he said, as he handed Ivy her drink.

With her nose scrunched up, she tasted it cautiously.

"I'm not much of a red wine aficionado," she admitted. "Tell me about it. I'm guessing this one's expensive?"

"It comes from the Rhône Valley in France. I've seen certain bottles go for upwards of four thousand dollars, but the vintage we're drinking is far more modest. What word would you use to describe it? Your first reaction…"

Ivy took another sip. "It's bold," she said. "Full-bodied. And I think I taste blueberries. Am I right?"

He lifted his glass. "Spot-on. But don't feel like you have to finish the glass. I won't be offended."

"It's very good," she said. "I seldom drink, though. I'll sip it, if you don't mind."

"Whatever you want. When our international guests are here, we'll have a wide variety of wines available. You can try them to your heart's content."

After that, the awkward silence came back.

Farrell drained his wine and poured himself another glass. "When Dolly woke up from her morning nap, you left me hanging," he said, keeping his tone light. "You wanted to leave your husband, but you found out you were pregnant. What happened next?"

Ivy shot him a sideways glance that could have meant anything. She set her half-empty glass on the table and rested her arms on the chair. But he noticed that her fingers clenched the upholstery.

"I know he did it on purpose," she said. "He thought if he got me pregnant, I wouldn't leave."

"Why would he believe that?"

"Because he knew how important family was to me. I missed my parents desperately after their deaths. Richard thought I would want my child to know his or her father."

"And did you?"

"Perhaps. But only for a moment. I became convinced that he would control our baby's life as he had mine, and that's when I knew I had to follow through with my original plan."

"So what did you do?"

Ivy stood abruptly and took a position in front of the fire, warming her hands. When she turned back to face him, her expression was tight with remembered struggle. "I hadn't counted on morning sickness. Brutal. Unrelenting. I lost eighteen pounds before I began to gain anything. I was so scared I would lose the baby. I threw up several times a day, and when I wasn't throwing up, I was so miserable all I could do was curl up in bed and sleep."

"And your husband?"

Her laugh was bleak. "He started traveling again. Two and three nights at a time. I barely had enough strength to force myself to eat. He knew there was no way I could summon enough energy to pack up and leave him. Unfortunately, he was right. And with every hour I stayed, I felt more like a failure. My daughter hadn't even been born yet, and already I was placing her in danger."

"You're too hard on yourself," he said. "You made it day to day. That's a lot."

"I suppose."

"Was childbirth as bad as the pregnancy?"

"Thankfully, no. Apparently I have good childbearing

hips." She chuckled quietly. "I was happy in the hospital. Everyone was so kind. And I had Dolly. She was this perfect little miracle. I prayed every day that Richard's DNA wouldn't harm her."

"Or worse. How did he respond to becoming a father?"

"It was very odd. Almost as if he didn't care. *I* was the one he wanted to control. Dolly was a peripheral in his life. He ignored her mostly."

Farrell wanted to stop right there. Ivy was fine. The baby was fine. And the husband was uninterested. It was a good place to end the story. But that didn't explain how Ivy ended up back in Portland, broke and alone.

He could almost see the toll it was taking on her to tell this story. Had she ever shared it with anyone? Unlike Farrell, Ivy's dark days were relatively recent. Was he helping her or hurting her by asking for the whole sordid tale? He honestly didn't know.

"Was your husband at the house when you came home from the hospital?" Farrell asked. "Or did he pick you up?"

Ivy shook her head slowly. "Neither. He'd left an envelope in my hospital room with just enough taxi fare for me to get home. That was typical. He didn't let me have a job, and he never gave me more than what was needed for a particular purchase. He often checked the grocery receipts."

"Wait a minute," Farrell said. "Even I know that hospitals won't let you go home unless a car seat has already been installed."

"That was another indignity. They made me meet

with a social worker. She asked all kinds of awkward questions. In retrospect, I might have been able to enlist her help in leaving Richard, but I had just given birth. I was exhausted and weak, and struggling to breast-feed. The timing wasn't right. Or at least that's what I told myself. I lied to the woman. Told her a friend was picking me up. With a car seat."

"But you actually went home in a taxi."

"Yes. I was lucky in one way. Over the years, I had been getting to know my neighbors on the sly. Because of that, some of them brought me meals and baby presents, including small amounts of cash. I was so touched. Richard did his best, always, to isolate me. But because he traveled, I had managed to make a few friends. Acquaintances really, but good people. I had to hide the gifts, of course. Richard came home when Dolly was one week old."

"Surely he bonded with her then. His own flesh and blood?"

"No. He complained if she cried. He insisted that I prepare his meals and do the usual chores. And then, I think, he realized that I was getting better every day. Recovering. Learning to handle the baby on my own."

"He felt threatened…"

"I think so. He must have sensed that my plans to leave—the ones he had destroyed almost a year before by getting me pregnant—were about to be resurrected. The atmosphere in the house was tense. I tried not to let Dolly know. When I was with her, I concentrated on being calm, focused."

Farrell held his breath. Ivy's story had slowed. It

was as if every word had to be forced from her throat. He stood to join her by the fire. "You don't have to say anything else, Ivy. I never meant to cause you pain. I was arrogant enough to think you should bare your soul to me. Because it would help. But instead, it's tearing you apart. I can see it on your face."

Her small smile was curiously sweet. "Your instincts were good, Farrell. And I appreciate the fact that you understand grief and loss. This thing that happened to me is part of who I am. I can't forget it. Telling you is no worse than what I dream about at night." She paused. "I'm not the woman I was before I left him. I've learned to trust my instincts. Fear doesn't control my life anymore. Being here in Maine with you has brought me peace and healing. This is more than a job for me. It's a new beginning."

He brushed her cheek with the back of his hand, barely a touch at all. "I'm in awe of your resiliency. You actually walked away. With a brand-new baby."

"Not exactly."

"Oh?"

Her bottom lip trembled. "New mothers aren't supposed to have intimate relations until their six-week postpartum checkup. Richard forced himself on me. After that, I developed a terrible infection. Had to be hospitalized. My milk dried up, because I was too ill to pump."

Farrell couldn't bear it. He pulled her into his arms and held her. That was all. Simply held her. His body registered the fact that a desirable woman was pressed up against him. But he was in control.

"My God, Ivy. It's a miracle you're even standing here with me."

She rested her cheek against his chest. He felt the shudder that racked her. "I know. They told me I could have died. Dolly was the reason I pulled through and went home."

He stroked her hair, sifting his fingers through the short, fluffy strands. "Who cared for Dolly while you were in the hospital?"

"I don't know." Her voice cracked. "He wouldn't tell me. I have no idea if she was happy or sad or hungry or inconsolable. I left her with him, because I had no other choice. Knowing that has eaten away at me."

"Look at her, Ivy. She's perfect. Whatever happened or didn't happen hasn't had a lasting effect. I've never seen a happier baby."

She sniffed, swiping her wet cheeks with one hand. "Thank you for saying that."

He pulled the hem of his shirt from his pants and dabbed her face. "So when you were well, you left him."

Ivy pulled back and looked up at him. Her long eyelashes were wet and spiky, but her color had returned. "You keep trying," she said, with a tiny grin. "But you haven't gotten it right yet."

"What? What happened?"

She played with a button on his shirt. "Ten days after I got out of the hospital, Richard had a massive heart attack. The one they call the widow-maker. The EMTs said he was dead before he hit the ground."

"Jesus, Ivy…" He was incredulous and horrified.

"So that was what? Five? Six months ago?" He'd done some quick math with the baby's age.

"Five and a half. I used the credit cards I found in his wallet. Paid for a private funeral. I had no idea who to notify, so it was just me and Dolly. When it was all over, I felt guilty, but overwhelmingly relieved. He couldn't do anything to hurt me ever again."

"Thank God."

"I began cleaning out the house so I could sell it. Nothing but bad memories lingered in that place. I didn't want to raise my baby there."

"How was the market?"

"The sale went through quickly. Dolly and I moved to a nice apartment near the university. I bought a stroller. We began going for walks in the afternoon. I knew I would have to get a job, but I wanted just a little more time with my baby first."

"Was there life insurance?"

"Yes, but not for me. As it turned out, Richard hadn't been traveling for work at all. Richard had been living under an assumed name in a town fifty miles away. He had another wife and two older children."

"Holy hell." This was a damn soap opera, and not a good one.

"The *other woman* knew nothing about me and vice versa. When her 'husband' disappeared, she hired a private investigator who eventually found the trail. And found me, of course."

"I don't know what to say."

"*Everything* ultimately went to her. Richard had a very basic will, with the other woman listed as beneficiary. They took all I had. Checking accounts, savings accounts, the credit cards, the proceeds from the sale of the house. Everything. The woman even demanded I pay back what I spent on the funeral and my living expenses in the meantime, but a judge intervened. He gave me five thousand dollars because he saw me as the innocent victim."

"Then how did you get back to Portland?"

"I mentioned to you that I had been subscribing to the Portland newspaper online for a long time. It made me feel closer to home, closer to the happy days of my childhood. Katie's sister placed an ad for a roommate. I saw it, and that was that. I bought an airline ticket and headed north. With only that small pot of money, I knew I had to make it last."

"Is that all?"

A tiny frown drew her brows together. "Yes. Isn't that enough?"

The hint of indignation made him smile. He lifted her chin, stared deep into her eyes. So much heart, so much everything. "You are the most amazing woman I've ever met, Ivy Danby. Incredibly strong. Resourceful. You've been bent, but not broken."

What happened next was not something he chose consciously. But no force on earth could have kept him from expressing what he felt…what her story had done to him.

He kissed her gently, trying to convey his utter admiration.

But from the start, the kiss was never in that column.

When their lips met, Ivy gasped. Or maybe it was

him. Didn't matter. Their souls connected for a moment. He'd told this woman things about Sasha that he'd never shared with another person. And by her own admission, Ivy hadn't had any confidants up until now.

Their shared tragedies had burned through several layers of social niceties and demolished a host of steps couples usually navigate in a relationship. Suddenly, they were deeply involved.

How had it happened? Farrell groaned her name and started to pull away, a knee-jerk reaction to his fear of intimacy. When Ivy leaned in and kept the kiss connected, her innocent pleasure seduced him. He was swept along by a dangerous current.

Like a calm ocean that conceals the treacherous undertow below, Ivy hadn't seemed a threat at all, until now. Abstinence wasn't the only explanation for Farrell's desperate hunger. He wanted *her*. Not just any woman. Her. Ivy had sneaked her way into his heart when he wasn't looking.

Damn it, he was lost. He cupped her face in shaking hands and tried to rein in his desire to gobble her whole. Her life story had made him angry and hurt on her behalf and utterly determined to show her how wonderful she was.

He took the kiss deeper, one heartbeat at a time. Always waiting to see if Ivy was with him. Her slender arms curled around his neck and clung. Her modest breasts pressed up against him, even as his hands settled on her hips and dragged her closer.

His erection was hard and urgent. He ached to fill her and please her and give them both what they so desperately needed. There was a sofa nearby. Hell, his bed was only a few steps down the hall.

"Ivy," he groaned. "I want you."

"I want you, too, Farrell," she whispered.

She kissed his chin, his nose, his eyebrows. Finally, she found his lips again. Her shy attempt at taking the lead twisted his heart and cracked it a little bit. When her tongue slid into his mouth and mimicked the kiss he had given her moments ago, his knees threatened to buckle.

"Wait," he said hoarsely, trying to regain control of the situation. "I never meant for this to happen."

Ivy jerked backward, almost stumbling. The stricken look in her eyes when he said those seven words made him hear how his protest might have sounded to her.

"I do want you," he said urgently. "But we have to be sure. And you have to understand the ground rules."

For the first time, she didn't look young and inno-cent. In her hazel eyes, he saw evidence of every time she had been struck down by life. He witnessed her res-ignation and her cynical acceptance of reality.

"No, Farrell," she said. "*You're* the one who has to understand. I gave up believing in fairy tales a long time ago. Farrell Stone is the prince in the castle, and I'm the girl down in the cinders trying to survive." She paused, her chest heaving. "Whatever *this* is…" She waved a dismissive hand. "I have no illusions. Am I interested in sleeping with you? Yes, damn skippy I am. But you don't have to worry. All I care about in this life is my daughter and her happiness. I don't need a man to cod-dle me or to protect me. My bogeyman is dead. So sleep with me or don't sleep with me. But do me the courtesy of understanding that I'm not a naive little kid. I know the score. I always have."

"That's quite a speech." Tension wrapped bands of pain around his head. Nothing about this was easy.

Ivy shrugged. "I believe in plain speaking."

"Then how's this?" he said, his jaw tight. "I want you, but I don't want to want you."

She flinched. Which made him feel like the worst kind of scum. Her chin lifted, and with careful dignity, she faced him down. "I know that, Farrell. You're still in love with your dead wife."

He wasn't. Not anymore. At least not in the way Ivy meant. But perhaps it was better for both of them if he let the lie stand.

While he struggled for a response, Ivy stared at him, gaze bleak. Then she turned and walked away. "It's time for me to take Dolly back to the cabin," she said over her shoulder. "Good night, Farrell. Thanks for the wine and the listening ear."

Ten

Ivy had never experienced such a wide range of emotions in such a short amount of time. Telling Farrell about Richard had been difficult. Extremely so. Because she still bore the shame and guilt about her part in losing a decade of her life.

But that was nothing compared to the exhilaration of being kissed wildly by Farrell Stone and then being condescended to as if she were some silly teenager begging for scraps of his affection.

She heard him on her heels and walked faster.

"Wait, Ivy. Wait, damn it."

She whirled to face him. "I don't need you fighting my battles or feeling responsible for me. The fight is over. I don't need you period." She glared at him. "Well, yes, for sex. But I can find anybody for that."

His eyes burned brightly. His lips pressed together in a menacing seam. "It's raining," he said. "I'll escort you and Dolly back to the cabin."

"Escort?" She gave him a derisive look. "What is this? 1840? I'm perfectly capable of getting wet in the rain."

Farrell took her wrist and pulled her close. The heat radiating from his body made her breathless. "I'm imagining it right now," he said, the words gravelly. Intense. "White skin. Raspberry nipples. Small, perfect breasts that fit in my hands."

The words mesmerized her. Heat pooled in her belly. Her knees pressed together involuntarily. "Stop it," she stuttered.

"Stop what?" He tangled his hands in her hair and brought his mouth down on hers. "Forget everything I said," he groaned. "This is all we need to talk about. And frankly, talking is overrated."

The kiss was deep and thorough. Ivy melted into him. Mortifyingly so. Where was her pride and her self-respect? She should slap his face.

But Farrell was so close and so perfectly masculine. And so gratifyingly hungry. His hands roved over her body, raising gooseflesh despite the warmth of the house. She wanted to jump into his arms and wrap her legs around his waist. Heat shot through her veins, dizzying and painful.

If he let her go, she would beg. She knew it.

But Farrell showed no signs of ending the kiss. He nipped the side of her neck with sharp teeth. Bit gently on her earlobe. Thrust one of his legs between hers.

They were both fully dressed. Her virtue was as safe as a nun's, at the moment. But holy hannah, she wanted him.

He was breathing hard when he finally released her. "I don't want to fight," he said, the words gruff.

She raised an eyebrow. "In other words, make love, not war?"

"It worked for an entire generation. Who are we to scoff?"

"Be honest," she said. "Did you ask me to sleep at your house during the retreat so we can have sex?"

"God, no." He stared at her, clearly outraged. "Why would I seduce you with a dozen people around?"

"Oh," she said, deflated. "I didn't think of it that way."

"I asked you for two reasons. I do need an official hostess, and I thought that you, as an outsider, could give me your perspective on how we present the company to our guests. I hoped the weekend would be fun for you, but that was a side benefit."

"Okay. I apologize."

"Go get the baby," he said. "We'll finish this at the cabin."

We'll finish this at the cabin.

Ivy parsed Farrell's enigmatic words as she gathered up the baby's belongings. Did he mean finish the conversation or finish this other thing they'd started?

Dolly was not happy about having her slumber interrupted. She was a warm lump in the port-a-crib. Ivy patted her back. "C'mon, love. I'll let you go back to sleep in just a minute." Ivy picked up her daughter and soothed her as she fussed. It was a bit late to realize that Ivy should have put on her own jacket first.

Oh, well. She wasn't going to freeze in such a short distance. But Dolly definitely needed to be wrapped up in a blanket.

Ivy met Farrell in the hall. "How hard is it raining?"

"Pretty hard. Let me carry her, so you can use an umbrella."

She clutched the baby. "You don't have to go with me."

His broad grin was unexpected. And it cut the sand from under her feet. "I'd like to, Ivy. If you don't object."

"It's your cabin."

He kissed her forehead. "But it's your home, and I won't intrude without an invitation."

Well, crud. Farrell was being a perfect gentleman. Ivy wasn't going to be able to call him out for pressuring her. "You're invited," she muttered.

His gaze heated, and a slash of red colored his cheekbones. "Thank you, Ivy. I accept."

In the mudroom, they donned rubber boots and rain slickers. The light rain from earlier had turned into a monsoon. "Watch your feet as we go," Farrell said. "Here. Let me have her."

When they opened the door, the wind blew in, bringing the scent of autumn rain and wet earth. The wild weather echoed the upheaval in Ivy's emotions. She stepped out into the black night…

Farrell was having fun. Traipsing through the driving rain with Dolly tucked up against his chest made him feel alive. Though he had long since recovered from losing Sasha, he realized in this moment that he seldom let himself do anything simply for *fun*.

Had he become a stuffy, nose-to-the-grindstone kind of guy? Did his brothers and his employees merely tolerate him? Did they roll their eyes behind his back and wish he would lighten up?

At the cabin, Ivy fumbled with the lock, opened the door and stripped out of her rain gear. "I'll put her to bed," she said. "You dry off. We should have both had umbrellas."

He handed over the baby. "I didn't trust myself to hold her one-handed. I'm not going to melt."

Ivy searched his face. For a moment, he thought she was about to say something. But she didn't. She simply left him standing in his wet clothes, feeling as if his world was tumbling around him.

When she was gone, he kicked off his shoes. Even his socks were soaked. The rain slicker had kept him mostly dry, but the bottoms of his pants legs were damp. What sounded good right now was a hot drink.

He was still rummaging in the cabinets when Ivy showed up in the kitchen. "Do you have any of those tiny marshmallows?" he asked. "I've made some hot chocolate."

"You're in luck," Ivy said. She opened a cabinet he hadn't gotten to yet and tossed him a plastic bag. "This Mrs. Peterson person who stocked the kitchen must know you Stone brothers well."

"She knows Quin. I suppose she may have picked up a few things about the rest of us." He poured two mugs of frothy hot cocoa and dumped a handful of marsh-mallows in his. "You want some?"

"Cocoa, yes. But I'll pass on the marshmallows."

"You're missing out," he teased.

"Okay, fine. Give me five."

"Five? Not four? Not six?"

"Too much sugar is bad for you."

Farrell eyed her thin frame. "An occasional indulgence is a good thing," he said mildly. "Makes life worth living."

He carried the mugs to the table and waved at her to sit down. Cradling the drink in his hands, he leaned forward and took a sip. He jerked back, muttering a word that made Ivy give him a pointed stare.

"You burned your mouth, didn't you?" she said.

"Maybe." He looked her over from her tousled hair to her hazel eyes to her soft, unpainted lips. "Quin's the impulsive one in the family, but I can take chances, too."

Ivy blinked as her face flushed from her throat to her hairline. "Is that what I represent to you? Taking a chance? That's not very flattering."

Farrell had attended upscale parties where scantily-clad runway models mingled with the crowd. Never once had he felt for any of those women the need to persuade. To possess. To conquer.

Yet with Ivy, he knew all those urges. "I don't know what this is," he admitted. "Do we have to name it? Analyze it?"

She sipped her drink carefully, and when she set down her cup, she had a rim of marshmallow residue around her lips.

Before Farrell could think it through, he leaned forward and licked away the sweetness. "You're welcome," he said huskily.

Her eyes widened. "I didn't understand you at first. I thought you were a serious scientist devoted to his work. But you're really a renegade, aren't you? A hedonist. A rascal."

Farrell gave her a lazy smile. "Isn't it possible to be all those things? Can't I want to sleep with a fascinating woman in my spare time?"

She reached out and covered one of his hands with hers. Her smile was shy. "I hope there won't be *much* sleeping involved. Surely we can do better than that."

His heart rate jumped. He twined his fingers with hers. "Don't toy with me, woman. I need an unambiguous answer. Do you want to go to bed with me? Here? Tonight?"

"I do. Rainy nights always make my imagination run wild. But we'd better get a move on, because you-know-who wakes up early."

Farrell followed her into the bedroom. He was as hard as his surname already, and he wondered if he had it in him to be gentle with her. But he must. Ivy had known too much male aggression in her short life.

As they stood beside the bed, he saw her confidence falter.

"Don't be afraid of me, Ivy."

"I'm not." She gnawed her lower lip. "I'm afraid you'll be disappointed in *me*. Richard messed up my head. I have a million hang-ups about my body. And I haven't ever…"

She trailed off, her expression anxious.

Farrell took her hand. "You haven't had sex with anyone other than your husband?"

"No." The single syllable encompassed misery and embarrassment.

"Then here are the ground rules," he said. "It's only the two of us in this room. No Sasha. No Richard. No painful past to bother us. Whatever happens between you and me is because we want each other. I plan to lose myself in making love to you, Ivy. I hope you'll do the same."

She searched his face, as if looking for evidence of his sincerity. At last, she smiled. "Okay."

Despite her whispered agreement, she flinched when he started pulling her top over her head. Though that tiny response bothered him, he kept his motions measured and careful as he undressed her. When she was completely naked, he threw back the covers.

"Get in and stay warm, Ivy."

"But shouldn't I…?"

He followed her train of thought easily. "I'll handle it this time."

When he made it down to his boxer briefs and stepped out of them, Ivy's eyes widened. She stared at his erect sex with a rapt expression that did wonders for his ego. Unlike many women, Ivy didn't try to be something she wasn't. She was like a baby swan, all small and fluffy and vulnerable to the dangers in the world.

"Scoot over," he said. "I promise to keep you warm."

Ivy curled up against his naked body immediately.

He took that as a good sign. She sighed deeply. "This is nice."

He choked out a laugh, aching with arousal. But he was determined to back-burner his libido if it meant pleasing Ivy. "More than nice," he said gruffly. He ran his hands over her smooth ass. "You feel so good, Ivy. I've been fantasizing about this."

She rose up on one elbow and stared at him in shock. "You have?"

"Of course. Men do that, you know."

"Women, too." She wrinkled her nose. "But you never once let on. Why not?"

"I wasn't sure it was appropriate. You work for me. I didn't want to take advantage of you." He hesitated. "To be honest, I still feel guilty."

"Don't be absurd." She snuggled into his chest again, patting his collarbone. "This job you gave me is temporary. We both know that. When the time is right, you'll go back to headquarters at Stone River Outdoors, and I'll return to Portland to look for another position. It's all good, Farrell. Besides, didn't we agree to focus on this room, this bed, this night?"

He kissed the top of her head. "You're right. We did."

"May I ask you something?"

Because he couldn't see her face, he wasn't able to analyze the odd note in her voice. "Anything," he said.

"I'd like to explore your body." She touched his nipple as if to clarify. "I want to learn what you like. What you want. Is that okay?"

Farrell didn't know whether to laugh or cry. Ivy's guileless request sent hot arousal coursing through his veins, searing him from the inside out. Could he handle Ivy's fairly inexperienced experiment? Did she not understand the power she held?

"Absolutely," he lied. "I'm all yours."

She began by kneeling at his side. Her breasts were small but perfect. When he tried to touch her, Ivy protested. "None of that. Put your hands behind your neck."

Already, his arousal was at fever pitch. But he obeyed. "Be gentle with me," he begged, not entirely joking.

"I love your body," she said softly. "It's so different from mine." She traced the shell of his ear, tugging at the lobe. When she leaned over and put both hands on his collarbone, he trembled. Her breath was warm on his cheek.

The look of fierce concentration on her face charmed and seduced him. She was so damn cute, so damn precious.

He bit his lip to keep from groaning aloud when she ran a fingertip down his sternum. His hip bones were the next stop on her erotic route. Then she scooted over between his legs, spreading his thighs, getting comfortable. His body went on high alert.

At first, she only looked. No physical contact. The fact that his sex was fully erect and oozing fluid seemed to enthrall her. She collected the drop of liquid on her fingertip and touched his lips. "Do you know what you taste like?"

She was destroying him. "No," he croaked. "Do you?"

"I'm about to."

When she took him in her mouth, he shook as if he had a terrible jungle fever. Though she was ostensibly in control, her innocent delight in learning his physical attributes made him snap.

With a muffled cry, he came, embarrassing himself and surprising Ivy. She wiped her mouth and sat back, her eyes wide. "Are you okay?"

He could feel his face turn blood red. "Damn, Ivy. I'm sorry. You make me lose control."

A frown settled between her brows. "I don't believe you."

He reared up, weight on his elbows behind him, and glared. "I'm a grown-ass man of thirty-two. I haven't jumped the gun like that since I was a teenager. You arouse me, Ivy. Don't you understand?"

She moved off the bed and grabbed a robe. When she had tied the sash so tightly even Houdini couldn't get into it, she backed up against the dresser. "You should go clean up. There are spare towels in the bathroom cabinet."

Just to annoy her, Farrell climbed out of bed and faced her, buck naked. He would bet a hundred dollars she wanted to look away, but his Ivy was a brave woman.

He stalked her, grinning. "Do you like what you see?" Already, his erection was being reborn. When Ivy noticed, her eyes widened.

"You're a nice-looking man," she said primly. "I won't dispute that."

"But?"

"You're arrogant. And bossy. And I'm not sure I want to have sex with you anymore."

"Oh, really," he drawled. "I think you're lying."

Her affronted expression was priceless. "And I think you're an oversexed Neanderthal."

"Don't move," he said.

One quick trip to the bathroom, and he was ready to pick up where they'd left off.

When he returned to the bedroom, Ivy still huddled in her terry-cloth armor. She apparently had too much pride to let him think she was scared. Which suited Farrell just fine.

He pulled her into his arms and kissed her roughly. "Last chance, Ivy Danby. It's my turn now. Do you want me or not?"

Eleven

Ivy was still stunned. Had she really aroused Farrell Stone to the point he lost control? That was what he wanted her to believe. Still, it seemed improbable.

When he wrapped his arms around her and kissed her as if she were his last chance at life, her knees went weak. Hot male flesh, lightly dusted with hair, felt alien against her smooth skin. Alien and delicious.

Farrell's body was a wonder. As a man in his prime, he had serious muscles and a body that was honed by hard physical labor. Though he had the funds to hire a hundred laborers, she had often seen him tackling demanding jobs outside the house.

He tugged a lock of her hair. "I asked you a question, Ivy."

"Keeping on kissing me," she begged.

"Not until you admit you want me." He made her yelp when he slid a hand between her thighs and entered her with two fingers.

Farrell groaned. "You're wet and hot, my sweet. Your body doesn't lie. But I need the words."

It was Ivy's turn to hover on the brink of orgasm. She shivered and ached and yearned for him to take her. "Please make love to me, Farrell. I want you. I want you to—"

He put his hand over her mouth, his laugh more of a strangled wheeze. "I'll take it from here, sweetheart."

Tackling the knot on her robe took longer than it should. But at last he had her naked again. Scooping her up in his arms, he managed the two steps to the bed and tumbled them both onto the mattress.

Ivy's skin was chilled. He pulled the covers over them and nuzzled her neck. He could think of a million and one ways he wanted to pleasure her, but those would have to wait. Tonight, missionary style needed to be enough. He didn't want to overwhelm her. He sensed that sharing a bed with him was a huge step for Ivy. He would do nothing to make her regret it.

Beneath the sheets, he found the flat plane of her belly with his right hand. Dipping lower, he touched her center and lightly stroked her clitoris. Ivy's keening moan raised gooseflesh on his body.

Incredibly, he felt his body yanking at the reins, racing toward the finish line again. Suddenly, he remembered what he had forgotten. *Hell.*

He rested his forehead on her belly, his lungs gasping for air. "I'm sorry, Ivy. I forgot the condom. It's in my pants pocket."

She opened her eyes, her gaze hazy. "Hurry."

The single feminine demand galvanized him. Moments later, he was back, pausing only to take care of protecting her. Then he picked up where he had left off. Her sex was swollen, entirely ready for him.

Yet, oddly, he needed reassurance. He scooted up beside her and drew her closer for a desperate kiss. "Are you ready, Ivy? I want this to be good for you, for us."

She kissed him back, one arm curled around his neck. "If you make me wait one second longer, I swear I'll poison your pancakes."

Her humor in the midst of his own sexual desperation made him gape, then chuckle breathlessly. She was incredible.

Calling on all the control he could muster, he moved between her legs and positioned the head of his shaft at her entrance. Though she arched and scratched and pleaded, he took her slowly, inch by inch, increasing the torment for both of them. At last, he was all the way in, his sex wrapped tightly in her feminine heat.

He could feel her heartbeat when he kissed the side of her neck. Shuddering, he pressed his cheek to hers. "You have a beautiful, perfect body, Ivy. Made for my pleasure and yours. Don't ever forget that."

Perhaps he still saw doubt in her eyes. She didn't answer.

So it was up to him to prove it. He twisted her nipple gently. A rosy flush bathed her face. Her skin was damp and warm, her body limber and responsive in his embrace.

When he scraped the furled nub with his fingernail, her pupils dilated. Her chest rose and fell rapidly. "Farrell…"

The drowsy pleasure he heard in those two syllables squeezed his chest, filled him with elation.

He moved then, one strong thrust, then another. Ivy cried out his name and arched into him. Small hands clutched his shoulders. Sharp fingernails scored his skin. Her climax went on and on as he reached between them and gave her added stimulation.

When he was sure she had wrung every drop of pleasure from her release, he let himself pound into her, blind with hunger, lost to reason.

In the end, he lost a piece of himself into her keeping. It terrified him, but there was no way to get it back. Ivy had stolen his obstinate refusal to live fully. Or maybe he had offered her his true self as a gift. Possibly the exchange had been unintentional on both their parts.

But the deed was done.

He closed his eyes and slept.

Ivy came awake in the dark, searching for what had awakened her. Automatically, she glanced at the baby monitor. But Dolly was sleeping peacefully. Then understanding dawned. The noise that had roused her was a gentle snore from the large man at her side.

She gulped and closed her eyes, trying to pretend she hadn't invited Farrell Stone into her bed. She might as well have coaxed a shark into the kiddie pool.

What had she done?

Lightly, she stroked his forehead, tucking aside the lock of hair that tumbled onto his brow. Moments later, the piece of hair was down again. In his sleep, he looked no less masculine, but far more approachable.

A heavy arm pinned her to the mattress, holding her just below her breasts. One of her legs was tucked between his. They were entwined like longtime lovers, not participants in a one-night stand.

Surely this was nothing more than that. Ivy had been lonely and hungry for physical contact. Farrell had needed to break his sexual fast.

She shouldn't make too much of this. But oh, how she loved having him to herself so intimately. His scent, a combination of warm male skin and something crisp and woodsy, marked her sheets.

Maybe she shouldn't wash them.

The clock read four thirty. She had at least another hour and a half before Dolly awoke. Carefully, she slipped from Farrell's embrace and made a quick trip to the bathroom. When she returned, her lover was half-awake, frowning that she was gone.

"Come back to bed," he demanded, the words husky.

"I was planning on it." He was a bossy man, for sure. But since their plans aligned at the moment, she wouldn't complain.

She dropped her robe on the floor and lifted the covers. As she climbed in, Farrell made a noise that sounded suspiciously like a growl. He dragged her under him, bit the side of her neck and paused only to ask, "More, Ivy?"

"Yes," she sighed. "Oh, yes."

* * *

The next time Ivy roused, it really was Dolly who interrupted her sleep. The alarm hadn't gone off, but on the monitor, she could hear her daughter's little morning noises.

Ivy stretched, feeling groggy and sated. When she turned to the other side of the bed, she found the sheets cold and empty. But there was a note. Brief and impersonal, but a note.

Dear Ivy,
I need to get to the lab. Don't worry about breakfast. I grabbed a banana from your kitchen.

Later, Farrell...

She frowned. *Later, Farrell?* What did that even mean? Her experience with "the morning after" was admittedly limited, but his blunt note wasn't exactly the stuff of romantic movies.

Then again, she and Farrell had been pretty clear about their expectations. He needed and wanted sex. Ivy had needed and wanted to feel normal again. Having sex with a man like Farrell meant she truly was healing.

Well, mission accomplished for both of them. No reason to feel sad or let down. Today was no different from yesterday. Life went on.

She would ignore the pain in the pit of her stomach that was evidence of bruised feelings. That wasn't an acceptable reaction to last night.

Because Dolly was still happy with her teddy bear at

the moment, Ivy dressed quickly and prepared a bottle before going into the baby's room.

Farrell might have left without fanfare, but Dolly was gratifyingly happy to see her mother.

Ivy changed the baby's diaper, put her in one of the cute rompers Katie had gifted them with and then sat in the rocking chair to feed her. Dolly had begun eating mashed bananas and Cheerios and a few other simple foods, but Ivy still enjoyed giving her a morning and bedtime bottle.

When Dolly's tummy was full, Ivy knew she couldn't delay going up to the big house any longer.

Though Farrell had waved off breakfast, he might come back for lunch since he hadn't taken a sandwich. Ivy decided to make vegetable soup. It was still cool and misty today. Soup would hit the spot.

She was nervous. Might as well admit it. How was she supposed to act this morning? Maybe she could take her cues from Farrell. For one crazy second, she contemplated walking over to the lab.

But no. They didn't have that kind of relationship. Besides, even if Farrell and Ivy had been a real couple, he had said more than once that he focused with tunnel vision when he was working on a project. He certainly didn't need interruptions.

The lunch hour came and went. She kept the soup warming on the stove just in case. Ivy ate and fed the baby. Put Dolly down for a nap in the study. Still no Farrell.

At two o'clock, she heard her phone ding, signaling a text. Farrell's communiqué was as terse as his pillow note.

Ivy, something came up in Portland. I'm there now. Will return with Katie and Quin tomorrow morning. Farrell.

She stared at the phone, feeling her heart shrivel in her chest. Was there really an emergency, or had Farrell left because he wanted to be clear about last night? That it was no big deal. Did he think she had the wrong idea?

Even worse, maybe he was feeling guilty for betraying his wife. Sasha hadn't intruded in the bedroom last night. At least Ivy didn't think so. But what if Farrell had awakened this morning and found himself grieving for the only woman who'd ever captured his heart? The woman he still loved.

The empty house and Ivy's depressing thoughts combined to steal the joy from the day. She had been so happy here. A new job. A new friend. And yes, Farrell *was* her friend, despite everything that had happened.

Perhaps he didn't have the same regard for her.

Would she have to leave? If one night in Ivy's bed had spooked him this badly, it was possible they could no longer coexist.

The prospect of going back to Portland was heartbreaking. She loved everything about Farrell's enclave here in the northern woods. Some women might crave restaurants and nightlife and excitement. But Ivy had never really known that kind of lifestyle. To her, this private getaway was idyllic. If she had kept Farrell at arm's length, the situation would have remained stable.

Now, because she had let her feelings get out of control, she might lose her job and her home and have to start over yet again.

To distract herself from her dismal thoughts, she climbed to the second and third floors to do one last reconnaissance. Though she touched up a mirror here and straightened a rug there, everything was in order. Farrell's guest rooms were lovely. Each one had an individual theme or color palette.

Clearly, some had ocean views and some looked out over the forest, but she couldn't imagine any guest complaining about *anything*. Luxury stamped each square foot.

She was both nervous and excited about the upcoming house party. Katie would be there to lend a hand with names or any of the million and one details that were bound to crop up. That was a comfort.

But why had Farrell gone to Portland?

What did it mean?

Instantly, she made a decision. Farrell would have no cause to regret sharing her bed. Ivy would make it clear from the outset that she was not emotionally involved… that she intended to move forward with business as usual. If she let him know by her attitude that nothing had changed, perhaps they could go back to what they'd had before. A cautious friendship.

Wednesday dragged. Ivy would like to say she didn't know why, but the cause was obvious. Farrell wasn't here to lend his passion and energy to the house. She missed him.

That was a problem. But she would deal with it.

She and Dolly spent a pleasant afternoon and evening together. Ivy went to bed early. The next four days would be busy and challenging. She needed her rest.

But her dreams were dark and disturbing. Farrell starred in all of them.

Thursday morning, she was at the big house early. Katie—not Farrell—had sent a text to say the three of them—Katie, Quin and Farrell—would arrive before lunch. Would Ivy mind preparing a light meal?

Of course Ivy wouldn't mind. It was her job, after all.

She jittered and watched the clock as she grilled chicken breasts and made a pasta salad. There were apples in the pantry that needed to be eaten, so she peeled and sliced them and threw together a fruit crisp.

Soon, the kitchen smelled delightful.

The sun had come out around ten, burning off the fog and drying out the surroundings. That was probably best when having foreign guests. Not everyone appreciated a rainy day the way Ivy did.

When she heard car doors slamming just before noon, she peeked out a window and saw the three adults climbing out of two cars. Her heart jumped and began to beat sluggishly.

Seldom did she have the opportunity to study Farrell unobserved. He looked even taller than she remembered. As she watched, he laughed at something one of the others had said. For a moment, he looked far younger than he was. This was the man Sasha would have known.

When the two Stone siblings and Katie entered the kitchen, Ivy was able to greet them with a smile. "Just in time," she said. "I hope you're hungry."

Quin dropped a briefcase in the hallway and stretched. "We got up too early. I'm starving."

Katie gave Ivy a quick hug. "Me, too. Everything smells delicious. May I help you?"

Farrell, noticeably, said nothing. He was flipping through a stack of mail in his hands. Perhaps that was his excuse for not acknowledging the woman he'd recently bedded.

Ivy nodded her head. "If you'll see what the men want to drink, the rest of lunch is ready." She took three plates and began doling out the meal.

Katie frowned. "Where is your plate?"

"I ate earlier," Ivy lied. "Dolly was up at the crack of dawn, so I was hungry already."

Katie seemed unconvinced, but she didn't press the issue.

Once Ivy put food on the table, she left the kitchen without fanfare and escaped to the study. Quietly, she opened the door and slipped inside. Dolly was still asleep, her little bottom up in the air.

Ivy sat down in a cozy armchair, leaned back and closed her eyes. She ached for Farrell, for the knowledge that he was giving her a wide berth. Had she ruined everything by sleeping with him, by giving in to the madness that had caught them up in a physical relationship that seemed inevitable?

Farrell had been so kind to her. So incredibly sexy. Was it any wonder that Ivy had a crush on him?

Being in bed with him, having him touch her and give her pleasure, had been an experience she hadn't known she needed.

With Farrell, she felt whole.

Twelve

Farrell handed Katie a sheet of paper. "Why don't you and Quin assign the rooms? I've penciled in a couple. I'll go find Ivy and see what else needs to be done."

As excuses went, it was clunky at best, but guilt burned a hole in his gut. How was he going to explain himself?

It took him several minutes to find Ivy. Only when he eased open the door to the study did he see the sleeping baby and her mother…also dead to the world. Or so it seemed.

Farrell slipped inside the room, closed the door silently and stood with his back to the wall. Watching the two females sleep made his chest ache.

Ivy hadn't heard him…yet. Either she was very tired, or the white noise of the fan had covered his quiet entry.

Until a few minutes ago when he walked into the house with Quin and Katie, he hadn't seen Ivy since he climbed out of her bed yesterday morning. Thirty hours, give or take.

It seemed an eternity.

He'd been an ass in the kitchen just now. His first glance at Ivy had knocked the wind out of him. Pretending to read the damn mail was all he could manage, because he hadn't known how to act or what to say.

At the very least, Ivy deserved an apology.

On the other hand, if he wasn't planning to sleep with her again, it would be best to pretend everything was normal. Could he do it? Could he act as if sharing Ivy Danby's bed hadn't been the best thing to happen to him in the last seven years?

After several long minutes—when Ivy didn't stir—he decided Fate was giving him a nudge. *Leave well enough alone. Water under the bridge. Never look back.* Any number of clichés came to mind.

Though his conscience and his heart were unsettled, he made himself slide to the left, reach behind his back, turn the knob and exit the room.

Katie tapped her old-school yellow legal pad with the tip of her pencil. "I think that's it. The caterer will be here at eight in the morning. She's sent me all of the weekend menus for approval. We have one vegan. One peanut allergy, and two gluten-free. I think we're in good shape."

Quin kissed the top of his wife's head. "Isn't she amazing?"

Farrell chuckled. "She was my admin long before she was your wife. I'm fully aware of Katie's credentials."

"Not all of them." Quin waggled his eyebrows and kissed the side of Katie's neck.

"Eww, gross," she said, shoving him away. "This is a *business* meeting, Quin. Try to be an adult, please." Her bashful smile took some of the sting from the rebuke.

"Yes, ma'am." Quin's hangdog expression was patently false.

Farrell stood and stretched. "Well, if you two lovebirds have everything under control, I think I'll hit the lab. Once the chaos starts, I'll be losing ground until Monday."

"How's the altitude-signaling device going?" Quin asked. "Any leaks?"

"None that I've heard of, which means there's a good chance the Portland lab really was vulnerable."

Quin sobered. "Zachary is trying to find an expert to analyze all the work computers."

Katie nodded. "But it sounds like a gargantuan task. If things are going well here, Farrell, I vote you continue working remotely until we know something for sure."

Farrell frowned. "What worries me is that we may *never* know."

Quin paced the kitchen restlessly. "If Stone River Outdoors has a corporate spy or a hacker or whatever they call it these days, we're *gonna* find out. End of story."

Farrell nodded. "I want to believe that. But the police don't have the manpower to pursue this. The suspect in your and Dad's car crash is dead. He was a drifter. A drug addict. And there's no evidence the crash was related to the theft of my designs, or that it was anything more than an accident."

"So we just drop it?" Quin's raw question held both anger and frustration.

"No," Farrell said. "As long as you and Zachary agree, I'd like to hire a private investigator."

"That will be damn expensive." Quin chewed his lip.

"But money well spent, right?"

"Yep. You have my vote."

Katie gathered her things. "I think an investigator is a great idea. But we have bigger fish to fry at the moment. Let's go to our house, Quin." She glanced at Farrell. "We'll be back at seven tomorrow morning. And what about Ivy?"

"What about Ivy?" Farrell tried to make the question casual, but Katie was eyeing him strangely.

She shrugged. "I wondered if you had filled her in on all the details, or if I need to do that?"

"I'm sure she'd appreciate anything you have to offer," Farrell said. "I think she's in the study with the baby. Dolly is usually awake by now. Feel free to check on them."

When Farrell strode out of the room, Katie glanced at her husband. "Was that weird?" she asked.

Quin rummaged in the cabinet for a new coffee filter. "Weird, how?"

"I don't know," Katie said, frowning. "They barely spoke to each other when the three of us arrived. I thought by now Farrell would feel comfortable with Ivy and vice versa."

"Katie," Quin warned. "It's not any of our business. You already made him hire Ivy. I think you've done enough."

"Hey," she said, hoping he was teasing. "It was the perfect solution."

"Maybe. But our Farrell is a certified hermit. Losing Sasha all those years ago changed him. He *likes* being alone. Having a live-in housekeeper and a little baby around may be wearing thin."

Ivy paused just outside the doorway, trying not to let on that she had overheard the entire conversation. Her face was hot and her stomach churned. Was it true? Had Farrell decided that peanut-butter sandwiches were preferable to having Ivy and Dolly underfoot?

Was he regretting the sex?

The hurt burrowed deep.

Half an hour ago, she'd been lightly dozing when Farrell sneaked into the study. She had snapped awake at the first tiny click of the doorknob. New mothers were trained that way. Any out-of-the-ordinary sound could be cause for alarm.

Holding her breath, she had waited for him to speak, thinking she would open her eyes when he did. Instead, he'd simply stood there and watched her. What thoughts had gone through his brain?

Perhaps he had come to tell her that this weekend would be the last of her duties. That he had changed his mind about needing a housekeeper. If so, why hadn't he done it?

Surely he hadn't come to talk about their momentary

indiscretion. Not that they'd been indiscreet, not really. Two grown adults. Single. Available. It wasn't as if the two of them had done anything scandalous.

They had each wanted and needed the other.

Dolly chortled loudly, meaning that Ivy could no longer hide her presence in the hall. Besides, this wasn't the time to analyze why Farrell Stone had made love to her like a movie hero and then shut her down cold.

Ivy cleared her throat, put a hand to her hot cheek and made herself walk into the kitchen. "Did I hear my name?" she asked cheerfully.

Katie looked stricken.

Quin smoothed the situation like a pro. "Katie was saying she needed to give you the update on our guests. Last-minute details. You know…"

"Oh, sure," Ivy said. "I need to know what you all want me to do this weekend."

Katie took Dolly and handed her off to Quin. "Grab her coat in the hall and walk her on the front porch for a few minutes, will you? Ivy and I need to put our heads together."

When Quin and Dolly exited, Ivy sat on a stool at the island. "Give me the rundown," she said.

Katie nodded and slid her notepad to Ivy. "Why don't you take a picture of this with your phone? It will help you keep the names straight. And the second page is all the dietary stuff. But the caterer has that under control."

Ivy frowned. "Your brother-in-law is paying me a generous salary. I feel like I should be the one cooking."

"Nonsense. He's been very clear. Farrell wants you as hostess."

"I've never done anything like that. My husband didn't even like to entertain on a small scale."

"That's the first time you've mentioned your husband to me," Katie said softly. "Are you handling things okay?"

Ivy nodded. "I'm fine. It wasn't a happy marriage, Katie."

"Oh." The other woman's eyes rounded. "I didn't know."

"No way you could have. I didn't even tell your sister when she advertised for a roommate. I was still processing Richard's death and what it meant for me and Dolly. Still am, I suppose."

Katie's gaze was filled with sympathy. "Would it make you feel better if I came to the cabin with you and we can choose outfits for the various parts of the weekend?"

Ivy exhaled. "Oh, gosh, yes. I've been agonizing over what to wear."

"Let me tell Quin where I'm going."

"Will he be okay with Dolly?"

"Of course. And if Dolly is her cute and charming self, perhaps she'll give my husband a few ideas."

Fifteen minutes later, Ivy unlocked the cabin with Katie right on her heels. Katie looked around with interest. "I like how you've settled in."

Ivy snorted. "If that's a polite way of saying we have toys everywhere, then yes. We're settled in."

Katie laughed. "It's organized chaos. I love it."

They made their way to Ivy's bedroom. Fortunately, Ivy had made her bed and tidied up that morning. "I've hung everything and pressed the wrinkles out of the few items that needed it. But there's so much."

Katie riffled through the hangers. "This for lunch tomorrow. First impressions and all that."

The outfit Katie indicated was a sophisticated black pantsuit with a teal satin tank beneath and matching jewelry. Ivy had a hunch that the necklace and earrings probably cost as much as her first week's salary.

The black leather flats were designer-made. The fact that she now also owned a half-dozen new bras and undies still made her shake her head in disbelief. "And after lunch?"

"The Stone brothers have planned a three-mile hike, nothing too strenuous. They want to show off the property and in the process demonstrate a few of our most popular pieces of outdoor gear. You saw that I ordered you hiking boots and trail pants that dry easily. You've got several options for tops."

"No wonder Farrell wanted a caterer. If he's going to take the group on a forced march, they'll be hungry."

Katie grinned. "Indeed." She held up a hanger. "I love this. It will be perfect for tomorrow evening. The men have planned for cocktails overlooking the ocean and then a formal dinner."

The dress Katie had picked out from a catalog had three-quarter-length sleeves, a curved neckline and a hem that came down to just above the knee. But when Ivy tried it on several days ago, the deep red silk clung to her body in such a way that every one of her curves, modest though they were, presented a provocative image.

Ivy hesitated. "It's awfully...*red*," she said.

Katie laughed. "Of course it is. And it looks amazing with your skin tone. It's really very modest. You can pull it off."

"Maybe there's something else a little less fitted?"

"Red for tomorrow night," Katie said. "No question. Hold your head up and be fabulous."

"I don't think *be fabulous* is in my repertoire."

"It's in every woman's repertoire," Katie insisted. "But sometimes we let ourselves believe the negative messages. From others and from ourselves. You're a lovely woman, Ivy. I'm sorry you had an unhappy marriage."

Ivy shrugged. "Maybe I'll tell you about it someday. Suffice it to say, Richard would never have let me out of the house in something like that. But *I'm* in charge of me now."

"All the more reason to shine. You're starting over, Ivy. Whatever the reason, crossroads in our lives are opportunities for growth."

Ivy smiled and sat on the edge of the bed, fingering the crimson fabric of the dress in question. "I'm beginning to see why you were the perfect person to bring Quin out of his funk. No wonder he fell in love with you."

"It wasn't me," Katie said. "I just gave him a nudge. Quin had to deal with the loss of competitive skiing on his own. Like any grief process, it took time. I'm really proud of him."

Ivy was envious of Katie. The other woman had clearly been confident *before* meeting Quin. From what Ivy had picked up, Katie had been running Farrell's R & D department back in Portland for several years. Now, though,

Katie glowed with the certainty of a woman who knew she was well loved.

"Okay," Ivy said. "We've picked out Friday's wardrobe, but how about the rest? I never knew there would be so many opportunities to change."

Katie turned back to the closet. "This top and pants for Saturday morning. More outdoor stuff for the afternoon, and the deep blue dress for Saturday evening."

Soon, between the two of them, they had Ivy's closet organized in the order she would need things. Despite a certain level of apprehension, Ivy was looking forward to wearing such gorgeous clothes.

When the task was done, they went in search of Quin. They found him in the kitchen letting Dolly pull every pot and pan and lid out of the bottom cabinets. Both women gaped at the mess.

Katie put her hands on her hips. "Quinten Stone. Your brother has a houseful of important company on the way in the morning. What were you thinking?"

Quin's grin was sunny as he kept one hand on Dolly's waist to keep her from tumbling into the open cabinet. "She wanted to. What can I say? I'm putty in her hands."

Ivy was more amused than Quin's wife. "She has that effect on me, too. Don't worry about it. I'll clean it up later." Quin was quickly becoming one of her favorite people. His mischief and charming sense of humor made him a delight to be around. Unlike his solemn brother.

Katie squatted. "We'll do it now. Sorry, Dolly. This is a big weekend. We all have to be on our best behavior."

Ivy spotted the legal pad on the counter. Something

on the housing list made her frown. "Why am I penciled in for the rose room? It's the nicest suite in the house. Oceanfront. King bed. That should go to one of our guests. I can sleep anywhere."

Katie and Quin exchanged a glance. Katie took the notepad from Ivy and glanced at it. "We're only using six of the eight upstairs bedrooms. Quin wanted you to be comfortable. He excluded the room with the twin beds at the back of the house and the bedroom with the smallest bathroom. The other guests are well taken care of, I promise."

Quin leaned against the fridge, letting Dolly play her favorite pull-the-hair game. "It's Farrell's house, Ivy. He calls the shots."

"But it doesn't make sense."

Again, the duo gave each other a look. It was Quin who spoke up. "My brother likes and appreciates you, Ivy. This is something he wanted to do. If I were you, I wouldn't make a big deal about it."

Ivy wasn't convinced. "Okay," she said slowly. She took Dolly from him. "The two of you should go. I've kept you too long. What time will you be back for dinner?"

Katie leaned her head on Quin's shoulder. "Actually, my husband is cooking me a romantic dinner for two tonight. You and Farrell will be on your own."

Thirteen

Ivy took Dolly to the porch. They waved as Quin and Katie climbed into their car and disappeared down the road. Now Ivy's last line of defense was gone and wouldn't be back until tomorrow.

Her stomach fluttered as she debated her options. Surely she and Farrell needed to clear the air before the house party. But how?

Holding the baby on one hip, she extracted her cell phone from her pocket and sent a text to her boss.

What time would you like me to have dinner ready tonight?

There. That was simple and straightforward enough. No hidden agenda. Farrell didn't reply to her text for twenty minutes. When he did, the note was not re-assuring.

I'll make myself a sandwich. Work is going well. I don't want to interrupt the flow. Why don't you and Dolly enjoy the evening?

Ivy frowned at the message, trying to read between the lines. The man was avoiding her. There was no other explanation.

This didn't bode well for the upcoming weekend, but short of dragging Farrell out of his lab and forcing a confrontation, she was out of options.

The impasse brought up something she had been thinking about recently. She and Dolly needed reliable transportation. Nothing fancy. If Katie and Quin would help her locate a used vehicle, Ivy had enough for a tiny down payment and regular payments.

Impulsively, she sent Katie a text to that effect. Then, because she felt guilty for interrupting their afternoon, she added a second note.

No rush on the car thing. We can talk about it later.

Katie sent a brief, cheerful response.

Afterward, Ivy was somewhat at a loss. The house was spotless. The boss didn't want dinner. Ivy might as well relax and play with Dolly…and later tonight, do her homework regarding the weekend guests.

Because she didn't want to risk the chance of running into Farrell again later—and because her stomach was growling—she popped Dolly into her high chair, pulled out a large wicker basket and began loading it with a few things. She would eat the leftovers from lunch as soon as she got back to the cabin. As for dinner, cheese and crackers and fruit would do.

When she had everything she needed, she managed to scoop up both the basket and her daughter. By the time she made it to the cabin, she was panting, not because it was a long way, but because a basket and a growing baby were an awkward handful.

She paused before unlocking the door to glance over into the woods. It was possible to see the roof of Farrell's lab through the trees. What would he say if she simply showed up on his doorstep?

She didn't have the guts to find out.

Having a chunk of the afternoon and all of the evening to herself should have been a lovely surprise, and it was. Still, the remainder of the day dragged. Babies were wonderful miracles, but any conversation with Dolly was one-sided at best.

Because Dolly had only managed a single nap today and not two, Ivy was able to put her daughter down by seven thirty. The poor thing was half-asleep while Ivy dressed her in one-piece pajamas and read her a book.

When Dolly was completely out, Ivy showered and washed and dried her hair. The T-shirt and knit pants she put on dated back to college days. After watching a movie that failed to keep her attention, she was just about to head for bed when she heard a soft knock at her front door. Unless the nearest bear family had developed human skills, her visitor had to be Farrell.

Her heart pounded. She could ignore the knock. The front of the house was dark. He would think she was asleep.

Sadly, no force in the world could halt her footsteps. No matter the cost, she wanted to see him.

When she swung open the door, his face was in shadows.

"May I come in?" he asked.

She hesitated, still trying to be smart. "Of course."

He followed her inside and waited while she turned on a couple of lamps. The room glowed intimately. When she turned around to face him, he took her wrist, reeled her in and buried his face in her shoulder with a moan. "God, Ivy. I'm sorry."

She stroked his hair, her eyes stinging. His torment was palpable. "It's okay."

He reared back. "It's *not* okay. I slept with you and disappeared." His indignation might have made her smile at another time. Not now.

"And why was that?" she asked gently, already knowing the answer. So she said it for him. "You felt as if you had cheated on your wife. I'm guessing that's been the case every time you've been intimate with a woman for the last seven years."

He ran his hands through his hair and paced. "That was true at one time. Not anymore. Or if it is, it's subconscious." His jaw worked. "I didn't leave your bed Wednesday morning because of Sasha."

"Then why, Farrell? And why were you acting so weird today when you and Quin and Katie arrived?"

He dropped into a chair, then leaned forward to stare

at the floor. When he finally looked up at her, the expression on his face told her that whatever tiny fantasies she had been weaving were dead in the water. Hopeless.

Shaking his head slowly, he drummed his fists on his knees. "I left because waking up beside you seemed natural. Good. But I can't do that, Ivy. I can't."

"Can't wake up with me?" She frowned. "I'm not sure I follow."

He rose to his feet again, shoved his hands in his pockets and stared at her, his posture rigid. "I can't care about you, Ivy. I won't. Not in that way. So for me to have sex with you is obscene."

She managed a smile though her heart was breaking. "It didn't *seem* obscene."

"This isn't funny." His tone was grim. "Losing Sasha nearly broke me. I swore I would never let myself care deeply about a woman again. I've lost my wife, my father and nearly Quin. I don't want to go through that kind of pain anymore. You and I have some kind of connection. I can't deny it, but I don't want it. And I certainly don't want to hurt you."

"But?"

"But I can't stop wanting you. It's eating me alive. What am I going to do about that?"

Did he really expect her to answer such a question? "It was just sex," she muttered.

He cocked his head, his gaze telling her he saw through the lie. "No. It wasn't. I'm guessing you wanted to know if you were still a sexually desirable woman. Or maybe you wanted to know if you had sexual feelings. I think we both found out the answer to that one."

"And you?" she whispered. Her hands gripped the back of a chair to keep from crumbling. "If it wasn't just sex, what was it for you?"

"I needed you," he said, the words flat. "Desperately, in fact. I hadn't been with a woman in almost a year. With my father's death and Quin's injuries, and then all the trouble at work, I had isolated myself emotionally. Told myself I could handle anything. But it wasn't true. You came along, and I began to want more. I wanted a connection."

"And yet you were deadly honest when you told me you didn't *want* to want me."

"I know." His gaze was bleak. "I'm screwed, aren't I? You should run far and fast."

Ivy shook all over. Her skin was icy. This moment mattered. Not only for Ivy, but for Farrell. How they went forward from here would send ripples into his future and hers.

"Here's the thing," she said, trying to sound reasonable and calm. "I've been through a bad time, but I'm good now. Or at least I'm headed in the right direction. Maybe one day I'll meet a guy who wants what I want, but clearly, that's not you. I need this job until I've saved enough money to move on somewhere else. You're so worried about using me or hurting me, but I know what I want. I'm capable of no-strings sex."

"I seriously doubt that."

He stared at her so long and so hard, she shifted positions restlessly.

"I am," she said. "I told you before. I'm no delicate, innocent flower. I've dealt with the good and the bad in my life, and I can tell you this—sex with Farrell Stone is good. But I respect your boundaries. You don't have to worry about me. I spent a decade married to a man who didn't love me. I have too much self-respect to repeat that pattern."

"You should have been a lawyer," he said, the grumbled words laced with resignation. "I'm not sure where I stand in this argument."

She held out her hand. "I forgive you for running away."

His lips twitched for real this time. "I did not run. It was more of a strategic relocation."

"Whatever helps you sleep at night." She withdrew her hand when he made no move to touch her. This sex-without-caring thing was going to be tough. "I can't compete with your sweet Sasha, Farrell. And I would never try. What is it that you want?"

He cursed, a tortured syllable echoing the corded muscles in his arms and the tension in his frame. "You know what I want."

"Yet you're still over there, and I'm over here. I don't need you to care about me, Farrell. I don't expect you to. All I'm asking for is a job and your sexy body. Fair enough?"

Slowly, he approached her. "When I first met you, I thought you were meek and mild. That's not true at all, is it?"

"I don't know. You tell me." She wet her finger with her tongue and traced his lips. "Does this feel mild?"

He scooped her up in his arms. "I don't know if I can handle a firecracker like you, Ivy Danby."

"Do your best, big guy."

* * *

Farrell had lost control of the situation the moment he knocked on Ivy's door. This little cabin had drawn him like a homing beacon. He'd been incapable of staying away. Though he had tried. God knew, he had tried. For the past two hours, he had dug through a box of Sasha's things, items he hadn't been able to get rid of for fear he might lose the last strand that bound him to his dead wife. Though her scent lingered in a treasured scarf, Farrell couldn't fully summon her image.

After seven years, Sasha was really gone.

Truthfully, Farrell had known and accepted that ages ago. What he hadn't come to terms with was being alone. As a deliberate choice. Because he didn't want to lose anyone else.

He carried Ivy carefully, set her on the bed gently. Inside, he was a raging mass of confusion and lust. A man in his condition shouldn't be allowed to make decisions.

The overhead light was off. A single lamp burned on the nightstand. Ivy's eyes were huge, rounded with a combination of apprehension and drowsy anticipation. The thin T-shirt she wore clung to her breasts, drew attention to her puckered nipples. The knit sleep pants outlined slender, toned thighs. A curvy ass. A narrow waist.

Maybe he should say something. The words wouldn't form. How did he explain something to Ivy that he hadn't come to terms with himself?

With jerky motions, he stripped off his clothes and rescued a strip of condoms from his pocket. He wasn't positive, but he thought Ivy blushed when she saw the condoms.

It was good that she was quiet. Earlier, that sexy, husky voice of hers had wrapped around him like warm molasses, making it hard to think.

"Scoot over, Ivy."

The bed was a queen, not a king. That was his fault. But then again, he hadn't been planning to sleep here when he furnished the place.

Under the covers, Ivy put a hand on his thigh. "Farrell?"

Her fingertips were almost touching his sex. Was that intentional? Was she trying to drive him berserk? "Yeah?"

"Before we start, could I ask you a question?"

He closed his eyes and willed his heart rate to slow. It wasn't working. "Sure," he croaked.

Ivy curled on her side, facing him. "Katie said you wanted me to have the beautiful oceanfront room on the second floor. I appreciate the thought, but I'd rather take that small bedroom on the back side of the house and let one of your guests have the suite with the view."

"You'll be working hard this weekend, and I—"

She put a hand over his mouth, stilling the words. Her smile made him dizzy. "Pay attention, Farrell. I'm asking if I can sleep with you at night. If you're concerned about appearances, I'm happy to put my things in a guest room, but I was hoping you and I could…" She trailed off, perhaps because he hadn't said a word.

His brain froze, analyzing her request. Trying to

subdue his strong reaction. His very positive reaction. "Sure," he said. "That would be fine."

Ivy blinked. Her gaze narrowed. "Fine? Well, never mind, then. It's too much trouble for *fine*." The pique in her voice was justified.

Farrell put his hand over hers. Over the small feminine hand resting on his thigh. "Touch me," he begged, pulling her arm to rest across his taut abdomen. "Hell, yes, I want you to stay in my room during the weekend. But right now, all I want is *you*."

The little gasp when he curled her fingers around his erection was Ivy's. Or his. Maybe both. He wasn't sure.

She must have finally recognized his utter desperation. Sliding down in the bed, she rested her cheek on his chest and sighed. "You have the most gorgeous body, Mr. Stone. I love how it's so different from mine."

And then she proceeded to touch every erogenous zone that sent his masculine libido into a frenzied state of high alert.

He wanted to complain when she abandoned his shaft, but having Ivy start at his ankles and stroke her way upward was its own kind of reward. After that, she skipped the high-dollar real estate and kissed his belly, his rib cage, his neck, his chin.

Then she settled on top of him, took his cheeks between her hands and kissed his mouth.

He shook like he had a fever. His hands grasped her butt, fingers digging into her soft, firm flesh. Ivy's tongue trespassed between his lips, stroking, turning him inside out.

Every inch of her touched every inch of him. She was draped over him like the perfect, sexy blanket.

But he wanted more. He needed more, or he might spontaneously combust. "Ivy," he whispered. "Can I have you now? Please?"

She pulled back and smiled, a cat-and-canary kind of smile that lit up her face and would have made him laugh if he hadn't been rigid with hunger. "Of course, Farrell," she said. "What are you waiting for?"

With graceless speed, he shoved her aside and reached for the protection. Moments later, he took about one-point-five seconds to decide. "On top," he grunted. "Hurry."

"Yes, sir."

It probably would have been less painful if Ivy hadn't helped. Her knee jabbed his hip; her foot nearly kicked his balls. At last, they were aligned as perfectly as planets in an orbital plane.

"Look at me," he said urgently.

Almost shyly, her gaze met his. "I'm looking."

His throat was tight. "I don't want you to have regrets," he muttered. It was the truest thing he had said. The words burst forth from some fount of wisdom deep inside him.

Her sweet Ivy-smile absolved him. "We're good, Farrell. Honestly."

Fourteen

Ivy knew she was headed for heartbreak. Knew it, and yet kept steering in the same direction. When Farrell entered her, she closed her eyes, concentrating on the exquisite feel of him. Inch by inch, he filled her, possessed her.

It was exhilarating and terrifying and, for her at least, earth-shattering. Richard had robbed her of so much. Now, at last, she had found her heart's desire. She loved Farrell Stone. More than she could possibly imagine loving any other man.

But he wasn't hers to keep. He never would be.

In this cozy bed, he made love to her with such passion and tenderness she wanted to cry. Feelings, so many feelings, rocked her, buffeted her.

Like a feather bounced on the winds of a storm, Ivy

took a journey whose destination she couldn't see. On the other side, tragedy awaited. It was a certainty. She was smart enough to know that.

Still, nothing could make her give up these next days of wonder and joy. Farrell rolled her beneath him without warning. Now he thrust forcefully, making her twist and groan as hot, sweet pleasure coursed from one part of her body to the next.

She wanted to make this moment last. Wanted to savor the time with him, this time when he was hers and hers alone, when she didn't have to share him with a ghost or even a houseful of guests.

But he was too good. Already he had learned her body. She felt her orgasm tingling in the wings. Farrell kissed the spot just beneath her ear, whispered hoarse words of praise. Ivy bowed up. Cried out. Tumbled over the edge of release and fell and fell and fell.

Until at last she rested in his arms.

They both slept.

Around two in the morning, Ivy roused. Farrell was sitting on the side of the bed, stretching. She put a hand on his warm back. "What's wrong?"

He leaned down to kiss her. "Nothing. Not a damn thing. But I just had an idea for the altitude beacon," he said. "I'm not running away, I swear."

She smiled, too sated and warm and lazy to be anything other than accommodating. "I believe you, Farrell. Go. This will be your last chance to work on it until Sunday afternoon or Monday—right?"

A tiny frown creased the space between his brows.

He stroked her hair from her face. "You really don't mind?"

"Not at all. Do what you need to do. Seriously." She took his hand, held it to her cheek and then kissed his palm. "I'm going back to sleep. I'll see you in the morning."

Farrell was exhilarated. He'd spent four straight hours in his lab fleshing out details that would make absolutely certain his invention worked as it should. The ideas had come thick and fast, almost more than he could keep track of as he typed and sketched and tweaked.

Leaving Ivy's bed wouldn't have been his first choice, but he had learned long ago that inspiration often showed up at the most inconvenient moments. Tonight, the experience of creating had been transcendent. He'd been jazzed, pumped, buzzing with energy.

After a shower, fresh clothes and a forty-five-minute nap in one of the armchairs in the study, he now floated on the caffeine from three cups of coffee as he prepared to meet the day. Katie and Quin showed up right on time, both looking sleepy. With them was Delanna, Katie's sister, who had arrived late last night.

The younger woman greeted Farrell. "Where's Ms. Danby? And the baby? I'm ready to start ASAP. Sis tells me all the guests will be here soon."

Katie dumped her enormous tote on the kitchen island. "Quin and I will meet the caterer and help her get set up. Farrell, why don't you take Delanna over to the cabin?"

Farrell was accustomed to being "handled" by his efficient admin. He nodded. "Of course. Come on, Delanna. Follow me." It didn't hurt that Katie's suggestion took him to the one place Farrell wanted to go.

At the cabin, Delanna and Ivy got reacquainted. "Thank you for coming," Ivy said. "I still feel bad about leaving you in the lurch. Have you found another roommate?"

Delanna nodded. "I did, and she's great. Cooks, too. Don't worry about it, Ivy. Things work out the way they're supposed to."

Farrell winced inwardly at that careless bit of philosophy. In his experience, "things" often backfired in your face, but he didn't contradict Delanna. Katie's sister was a free spirit. Who was he to judge?

When Ivy finished going over Dolly's schedule and handed off the baby to her new sitter, Farrell pulled Ivy aside. "You look fantastic," he said, wanting to kiss her, but certain she would object in this situation. She wore slim-legged black pants with a matching jacket and a silky top whose color reminded him of the ocean at Martinique.

Her smile lacked conviction. "Thanks. I'm nervous," she confessed. "Katie had flats picked out for this outfit, but I went with the heels instead. Feeling taller gives me confidence."

He let his gaze drift from the silky wisps of hair that brushed her forehead to her flushed cheeks to the rise and fall of her chest. "Just be yourself, Ivy. All I need you to do is analyze the way we handle this get-together. Take note of anything you think should be altered or eliminated. Your insights will be important when we do an evaluation later."

"You make it sound so easy. This is my first billionaire house party. I won't know what to say."

He cocked his head, giving her a devilish smile. "*I'm* a billionaire," he said. "You seem to have plenty to say to me. Remember?" He mimicked her voice. "'Ooh, there, Farrell. Don't stop. More, harder, faster.'"

Ivy's face turned beet red as she glanced around frantically to see where Delanna had landed.

"Relax," Farrell said, chuckling. "She and Dolly went out the back door to look at the birds."

"Oh." Ivy put both hands on her hot cheeks. "That wasn't funny."

"Pretty funny from where I'm standing." He kissed her cheek, careful not to muss her hair. "You smell delicious. Do we need to take your suitcase?"

"I'll get it later when I change for the afternoon. I'm ready to head up to the house."

By the time they returned from the cabin, the caterer had taken over the kitchen. Katie and Quin had been banished to the front hallway. And the first of Zachary's caravan of limos had pulled up in the driveway.

The next half hour was organized bedlam. The introductions alone took forever. After everyone had met everyone, the three brothers—plus Katie and Ivy—began ushering couples to their various rooms.

Farrell kept an eye on Ivy, curious to see how she would react to the diverse group. But he needn't have worried. She plunged right in, chatting and listening, and offering help when it was needed.

The large dining room, a place Farrell seldom used except for weekends like this one, was already set up for the luncheon. When he checked on the caterer, the pleasant thirty-something woman gave him a thumbs-up.

By the time the crowd had raved about the view, freshened up and rested if necessary, Farrell already had a good feeling about his goals for the weekend. He and his brothers and Katie took one last look at the packets they would be passing out after the meal.

The navy folder with ecru lettering and the SRO logo—two mountains intertwined with a river—was filled with glossy, impressive images of the company's latest products, many of which would hopefully be adopted by the guests and their respective companies.

Everyone had been asked to convene in the dining room at eleven thirty. When Farrell walked in, he found Ivy chatting animatedly with the only "single" guest on the roster. Unashamedly, Farrell lingered behind the open door and listened.

Ivy laughed. "I'm serious," she said. "When Farrell told me a Swiss watchmaker was coming, I pictured a stooped old man with a long white beard and tiny gold spectacles. You're not at all who I pictured."

Luca Bain took her hand and kissed it with European flair. "I hope you are not disappointed, mademoiselle."

Farrell bristled unconsciously. The sophisticated, well-traveled bachelor was easily twice as wealthy as the Stone brothers. And he collected female hearts as a hobby—never in one piece. Until this exact moment, Farrell hadn't thought about the fact that Ivy might be vulnerable to Luca's suave charm.

Ivy blushed at having her hand kissed. Women loved that kind of thing. Farrell's misgivings grew.

She escorted Luca around the table. "I believe you and I are seated here by the window. And you speak French? Again, not what I expected. I would have guessed a German accent."

"My people are from western Switzerland," Luca said. "Our country has four national languages. Where I live, it is not uncommon to hear French."

The conversation continued, but Farrell was forced to abandon his spy post and greet his other guests. In addition to the Swiss playboy, the Italians had brought their twin nineteen-year-old daughters, whose presence evened out the numbers.

Farrell couldn't very well insist on sitting beside his lover. He and his brothers, along with Katie and Ivy, were spread around the table. Katie had found someone at the Portland office who was proficient in calligraphy, so the place cards were works of art. When everyone was seated, Farrell greeted the group on behalf of Stone River Outdoors and expressed his appreciation.

"We're delighted you're all here," he said. "Our hope is to show you a relaxed, enjoyable weekend…one where we can all get to know each other and hopefully make plans for our collaboration." He picked up his wineglass. "To future endeavors. May they bloom in each of our countries."

Ivy beamed at Farrell. She might be prejudiced, but she thought he was the most impressive male in the room. He had a natural air of command and, when he put his mind to it, a warm, welcoming attitude that made people feel at home in his gorgeous house.

Luca Bain, at her right hand, tried to monopolize her attention. He was handsome, probably *too* handsome. A little full of himself. At the appropriate moment, Ivy directed her attention to the gentleman on her left. The Namibians, native Africans, were an impressive couple. Tall and reserved, they spoke perfect English with a delightful accent.

Their safari company was one of the top three tourist businesses on the entire continent of Africa. Most of their clientele was European, so their impetus for traveling so far was to work with Stone River Outdoors and hopefully grow their client base in the US.

When lunch was done, the schedule allowed for an hour of free time before the afternoon's planned activity. Zachary pulled Ivy aside in the hallway. "Thank you for all you've done for my brother."

Ivy evaluated that statement and decided there was no way he could know about the sex. "Honestly, I should be thanking the Stone brothers. I was at a low point in my life. Needed a job. Katie vouched for me. Your company is paying me well to be helpful."

"Still," Zachary said. "Knowing you've been here to look after Farrell has given the rest of us peace of mind."

She frowned at him. "Your brother is a grown man. He hasn't needed a babysitter."

"I didn't mean it like that." Zachary lowered his voice. "He lost his wife some years back, as I suppose you know. It hasn't been easy. We love Farrell, but we worry about him disappearing into that damn lab and never coming out." He shrugged. "I've always looked up to my big brother. I want him to be happy again. But in the meantime, I'll settle for well-fed and not a vampire."

Katie interrupted. "Ivy, do you mind helping me with the snacks?"

Though the international visitors had some downtime, the rest of the group was busy constantly. Quin would be taking point on the hike. He and his siblings were providing brand-new backpacks and personal hydration systems for each guest.

After the fresh-squeezed orange juice and homemade granola bars were packed, Ivy rushed over to the cabin to change clothes and retrieve her suitcase. She had folded all of her new clothes carefully, and she wasn't going far. Delanna was reading a book while Dolly napped.

"I'll be here at eight to put her down for the night," Ivy said.

"Won't that be in the middle of your fancy dinner?"

"I'm sure they won't miss me."

By the time she made it back to the big house and climbed the stairs to the second floor, she was hot and flustered. Taking the smallest bedroom at the back of the house only made sense. And besides, it was only "less" desirable in comparison to the other rooms. The furnishings and decor were actually quite lovely.

She felt a little self-conscious in her new hiking gear. The price tag on the shirt alone made her gasp. Nothing but the best for the Stone family. And Ivy, it seemed.

Everyone had agreed to meet out front at two thirty. Ivy made it with three minutes to spare. Farrell frowned at her from across the porch. She wrinkled her nose at him and turned her back. He wasn't the one juggling two residences and a baby and a distinct lack of experience with social occasions.

The group set off through the woods with much chatter and enthusiasm. Each of the Stones' visitors was widely traveled and widely experienced in high-end physical challenges. The Italian couple, in their late fifties, had made their fortune in the wine business. Now their walking-tour company was more of a retirement hobby, or so they claimed. Katie had told Ivy they had a seven-figure income *solely* from Tuscany Travels.

It was the same for the expat Irish couple who did ecotours in the British Virgin Islands.

Only Luca Bain was a bit of a puzzle. He'd been around the world, too. Had skied with Quin and raced Formula One cars with Zachary. He and Farrell climbed together in the Alps.

Even the Italian daughters were more cosmopolitan than Ivy. One had already begun an international modeling career, and the other was entering university in the spring, with plans to become a doctor.

Ivy was relieved to know she was able to keep up with the pace. Although this kind of trek was not something she normally did, she had exercised diligently after Dolly was born, and her body was fit. Because she had been so ill during her pregnancy, she'd not had as much baby weight to lose as some women.

The trail wound through the woods and up over a rise to a promontory overlooking the ocean. A breeze blew off the water, cooling heated skin. As everyone paused for a drink, Quin gathered the troops and gave them a quick, humorous summation of Stone family history.

They were standing on the northernmost point of their ancestor's land acquisition. He grinned. "I know you're all jet-lagged, but since you'll probably wake up early tomorrow, I recommend the sunrise. We're so far east in the continental United States, we catch the morning rays before any of our other countrymen. My great-grandfather always used to say that was why Stone River Outdoors prospered."

Katie joined Ivy at her elbow. They were standing at the back of the group, listening and watching. Katie sighed. "Isn't my husband wonderful?"

Ivy laughed softly. "He is, indeed. But Quin is the lucky one, because he found you. You're the perfect couple."

"I hope so." Katie sobered. "I worry that he'll get restless or bored with me. His life has been one adventure after another. As a single man with unlimited funds, the world is a smorgasbord of entertainment and experiences. Do you think he'll be able to settle down to domesticity?"

"Aren't you the one who told me to forget about the money? To jump right in and be fabulous? You're going to have a wonderful life together, Katie. The man adores you. He wants to be with you."

Unlike Farrell and Ivy. Farrell wanted sex with Ivy, but not a relationship. He couldn't have been clearer. Though her chest ached with poignant regret, she told herself to enjoy this time in Maine. It wouldn't last forever.

Amid the flurry of activity after Quin's speech, Ivy stepped closer to the edge of the small cliff, closer to the ocean. She'd spent half her childhood in Portland, the rest of her life near Charleston. Always, the sea had been a pull in her life.

Ivy was determined to make the next decade a memorable one. In her gut, she knew that leaving Farrell, losing him, would be a blow. But she was stronger now than when her parents died. Ivy would not be that vulnerable again.

She and her daughter were a family. Ivy wanted to give Dolly the kind of childhood here in Maine that she herself had experienced. The state was plenty big. She could stay out of Farrell's way.

She sneaked a peek at him. With the sun burnishing his hair and the breeze carrying his masculine laughter, he seemed like a star, a man far out of her reach. He was flesh and blood. That much was true. But billionaires didn't marry destitute widows with babies.

Maybe if she told herself that enough times, she would believe it.

Fifteen

Farrell nursed a cup of coffee while leaning against the front-porch railing of his house Saturday afternoon and brooded. Even the brilliant robin's-egg azure of a cloudless sky and the serene expanse of darker blue sea hadn't eased his mind. Parts of this weekend had skidded off track in the wrong direction. But that was personal, not business.

As far as Stone River Outdoors was concerned, the corporate retreat, or house party, or whatever you wanted to name it, was a success. He and his brothers had called an audible last night and changed up the plan with the caterer's permission. Instead of a formal dinner in the dining room, they had set up tables on the porch to take advantage of the near-idyllic weather.

Zachary had fired up two gas grills to cook bison

burgers and chicken. The caterer then prepared all sorts of delicacies and served them alfresco. Katie suggested s'mores and made a not-so-quick dash for ingredients. Quin built an after-dinner bonfire. Farrell's sophisticated guests took to the distinctly American treat with enthusiasm.

But it had been a late night when all was said and done. Everyone was exhausted. Though Ivy had slipped away to put Dolly to bed, she returned as promised. Even then, she eluded Farrell's attempts to have a private conversation with her. Earlier, she had said she wanted to sleep in his room, but instead, she had excused herself when the Italian twins headed upstairs. She joined the two young women on the pretext of helping them find a TV program they wanted to watch. But she didn't return.

Perhaps Ivy was having second thoughts.

This morning, breakfast had been a riotous affair. The group was becoming more cohesive, which was part of the point of this exercise. During a two-hour brainstorming session before lunch, led by Zachary, Quin and Farrell, the guests had been enthusiastic and connected as everyone discussed ways to build reciprocity in their business relationships.

Ivy did not attend, which was fine.

But she had been there at the noon meal when Luca Bain snagged a seat beside her and wielded his European charm. Farrell couldn't tell if Ivy was affected by Bain's determined flirtation or not. But in this kind of situation, anything was possible.

During the afternoon's expedition—sea kayaking

down at the tiny beach—Ivy had actually shared a kayak with Zachary, who professed himself more than happy to give the inexperienced Ivy a few lessons in how to paddle.

Farrell ended up with one of the gorgeous Italian twins in *his* kayak. The girl was funny and charming and game to try this new sport, but although Quin teased Farrell on the sly about his lovely companion, Farrell had no interest in a nineteen-year-old. The only woman he was focused on was Ivy. And she had clearly been enjoying herself with Zachary.

This was what happened when a man mixed business with pleasure.

Tonight's meal was formal. Farrell would be forced to shower and shave and don his best dark suit. But he made a decision on the spot. Ivy would sit beside him.

As he turned to go back into the house, something in his chest caught. Ivy was standing there. Watching him.

He cleared his throat, his grip tightening on his empty stoneware mug. "How long have you been out here?" he asked.

Her tiny smile was shy. "A bit. I like watching you," she said. "Especially outside. The sun catches the gold in your hair."

The innocent compliment made his face heat.

Before he could respond, Ivy joined him at the rail. "We've been so busy since you left the cabin Thursday night, I haven't had a chance to ask you about the device. Did you make progress? I know you were operating on very little sleep yesterday. I hope the lab time was worth it."

He inhaled her light, feminine scent, feeling his mood shift in a positive direction. Something about being with Ivy smoothed his rough edges. He knew it would embarrass her if he mentioned it, but her slow, sexy speech affected him strongly. Always had. Even that very first day.

Perhaps it was why he had hired her.

He set the mug on the rail, resisting the urge to pull her into his arms. They were surrounded by a dozen other people, even if none of them were close at the moment. Discretion was advisable no matter how badly Farrell wanted to hold her and kiss her.

"The weekend is going extremely well." He cleared his throat, fully aware that he wasn't saying what he wanted to say. "Thanks for everything you've done."

"Happy to help," she said. "They're a fun bunch of people."

The afternoon was unusually warm. Ivy was wearing another of the outfits Katie had picked out. The turquoise cotton dress with yellow polka dots bared Ivy's arms and emphasized her narrow waist. Yellow-and-gold sandals completed the look.

With her short haircut and delicate jawline, there was an innocence about her, a sweetness.

But in bed, alone together, Farrell had discovered another side of his prim Ivy. She was fire and heat when he made love to her. Her body was strong and sensual, drawing every bit of his hunger to the fore and then drowning him in blissful completion. Each time was better than the last…which gave him high hopes for tonight.

"Will you come to my room later?" he asked, the words barely audible, though he could just as easily have traced the shell of her ear with his tongue and whispered the invitation.

They were facing the ocean, shoulder to shoulder. Quickly, he touched her hand, tracing the bones in her wrist. Even that simple connection made his skin hum with need.

He needed privacy. "Will you, Ivy? You disappeared last night."

She shot him a glance, wrinkling her nose. "It was awkward. And late. And did I mention awkward?"

Her humor made him smile. "I understand. And to be clear, I could come to your room if that would make you more comfortable."

"No," she said quickly. "Downstairs is private. I'll come."

He bumped her hip with his. "Oh, yes, you will," he said quietly. "I'll make sure of it."

"Farrell!" Ivy looked behind them to make sure nobody had stepped outside.

"Relax," he said. "I wouldn't do anything to embarrass you, I swear." He squeezed her hand gently and then stepped away three paces, giving her a rueful grin that made him look like a sexy bad boy. "Once we're behind closed doors, though, all bets are off."

The heated certainty behind his teasing words made her stomach flip. Despite the fact that she had told Farrell she wanted to share his bed, she'd kept her distance from the "boss" since his guests arrived. She didn't need *anyone*, especially Farrell's family, to get ideas.

She yearned to be with him, but she was conflicted.

What Ivy and Farrell shared in private was theirs and theirs alone. It would go no further than this interlude in the Maine woods. No rosy future beckoned. But that didn't make her time with Farrell any less special.

Ivy felt the wind ruffle her hair. The new clothes were not so strange now. She no longer felt like a kid playing dress up. Katie had been right in that regard. When Ivy made the choice to relax and enjoy her flattering new wardrobe, the decision had given her self-confidence a boost.

The international guests had been a surprise in many respects. Ivy thought most of them would be high-maintenance. That they would demand and expect preferential treatment. A certain level of deference.

Instead, they had been—to a person—delightful.

It was possible Ivy had a chip on her shoulder about the wealthy. This weekend, her prejudices had come smack up against reality, and she'd had to make adjustments. Still, there were moments. Like when Farrell told her that Luca's company sold a couple of watches that retailed for two hundred grand apiece.

The zeros made her mind boggle.

"I should probably go change," she said. The words were wistful. These few moments with Farrell were precious. She ached for him. Avoiding a tryst last night had been nothing more than cowardice on her part. She wouldn't make that mistake again. "So dinner's at seven?"

The look he gave her threatened to melt the polar ice caps and turn her into a puddle. "I'd like to skip the stupid dinner and take you straight to bed. It's been almost forty-eight hours, Ivy. Why do you torture me?"

She started to make a flip comment until she saw that he was apparently in earnest. Not joking. At all.

"Umm…" What did a cautious woman say to that? "I want you, too," she whispered.

Farrell's face flushed. His eyes glittered. "Go inside, Ivy. Please. Before I do something reckless."

Farrell was ready for the weekend to be over. But he still had to make it through lunch on Sunday before he could say goodbye to his houseful of guests. After the days of peace and quiet with only Ivy and Dolly for company, his tolerance for strangers, amiable though they were, was waning.

It didn't matter that SRO business had gone spectacularly well. Or that his guests had been intelligent, charming and helpful. He was done. He wanted to be alone with Ivy.

As the crowd gathered for the evening meal, he watched the door for her. Already, champagne flowed like water. Tonight's mood was celebratory. The caterer, with a bit of help from Katie and Ivy, had dug out china and crystal and an enormous Irish linen tablecloth that was specially made for this table.

Katie had arranged for a florist to bring fresh flowers, pumpkins and gourds to mark the season. Large potted mums in yellow, bronze, magenta and white decorated the foyer, the hallway and corners of the dining room. As a centerpiece, the same florist had created a long, low arrangement of eucalyptus, baby pine cones, tiny white asters and several shades of moss interspersed with white votive candles.

Farrell was no particular judge of botanical creativity, but even he thought the table looked particularly beautiful tonight. It made him think of a mystical fairy forest. The whimsical thought ground to a halt when Ivy finally entered the room.

"Good God," he whispered reverently.

Katie was standing close enough to hear him. Her smile was smug. "I did well, didn't I?"

"I'm not sure," he muttered. Luca Bain was already making a beeline for Ivy. "We need to keep that Swiss lecher away from her."

Katie pooh-poohed him with a frown. "Luca is a lovely gentleman. Ivy is a grown woman. She can decide who she's interested in and who she's not."

"This is a *work* weekend," Farrell said, hearing his own truculence and unable to stop himself.

"Don't be absurd. The work is done. It wouldn't hurt Ivy to enjoy herself tonight. She's had a tough few months. If Luca wants to entertain her, what's the harm?"

Katie moved away to chat with one of the guests.

"Over my dead body," Farrell muttered. But he couldn't make his feet move. So he simply stared at her. At Ivy, that was. His Ivy. His sweet, unassuming, gorgeous Ivy, who looked beautiful to him no matter what she wore.

Unfortunately for Farrell's peace of mind, Ivy was dressed to kill tonight. Though the bodice and hemline of her fire-engine-red frock were modest, the cut of the dress left little to the imagination. It accentuated her small breasts and flattered her narrow waist and heart-shaped ass.

And those legs. Those legs.

He gulped his champagne, hoping to ease his parched throat. Only sheer force of will kept his erection at bay.

Honestly, there was nothing prurient about the red dress. But for a man who was ass-over-heels in lust with Ivy, it was the equivalent of waving a crimson flag in front of a raging bull.

Three hours, Farrell told himself. Three hours, and everyone would go upstairs to bed. Except for his Ivy.

The meal was exquisite, the guests complimentary. The caterer glowed. Interesting conversation rippled back and forth across the table.

If anybody had been keeping score, they would likely rank this as one of the best damn dinner parties in the history of dinner parties.

All Farrell could think about was how soon it would be over.

Dessert was generous slices of pecan pie slathered with recently whipped cream. Farrell was so far gone he debated asking the caterer to leave any leftover whipped cream in the fridge. So Farrell could use it later. To decorate his lover's body as he kissed her from head to toe.

In the midst of his lust, reservations lingered. He was getting in too deep with Ivy. He couldn't let himself get attached…or wish for more. To lose someone he cared about—again—would cripple him. No relationship was worth that kind of pain. He'd convinced himself he could handle a light, fun physical relationship. But what if he was wrong?

He loosened his tie and told himself no one ever died of sexual deprivation. Suddenly, he lurched to his feet, determined to move things along. Ivy was seated between the Irish husband and the Swiss watchmaker.

Farrell had not been able to rearrange the place cards at the last minute, so *again*, he wasn't seated with Ivy.

He extricated her suavely. "Could you help me with something in the study, Ivy?" He gave both men a genial smile. "We won't be long."

Ivy stood and followed him. In the hall, she gave him a puzzled look. "What was that for?"

Privacy, Farrell thought desperately. He needed privacy. Taking Ivy by the wrist, he pulled her along to the study. Once inside, he locked the door. Slowly, he backed her up against the wall.

"That dress," he grumbled.

She glanced down at herself. "I was supposed to wear this last night, but when you all decided on the more casual event outside, I went with the blue instead. What's wrong? Did I spill something on myself? I hope not. This silk is dry-clean only."

He placed his hands, palms flat, on either side of her head. "You didn't spill anything." His gaze settled on her full, rosy-red lips. The lip stain she wore must have been semipermanent, because the meal hadn't removed it.

His chest rose and fell with the force of his ragged breathing. "I'd like to kiss you," he said, the words ridiculously formal.

Ivy's eyes rounded. Perhaps only now did she understand the true nature of their errand. She licked her lips. "I thought we were waiting until later."

"Can't," he said gruffly. "That dress."

Slowly, he reached out and cupped one of her breasts. He gave her plenty of opportunity to say no…to shove him away.

Instead, she smiled. "Patience, Farrell. Good things come to those who wait."

"Says who?" He leaned his forehead against hers. "Let's go to your cabin," he muttered, only half kidding.

Ivy stroked his hair. "Dolly and Delanna are there… remember?"

He groaned. "Hell. I'm the only man I know who can build a fortress of solitude in the middle of northern Maine and still not find a quiet place to kiss a girl."

"I'm a woman, Farrell." She cupped his face in her hands and kissed him. Slow, sweet, hot as a firecracker.

The taste of her exploded on his tongue, sent urgent messages to his sex and all other stops along the way. He pulled her tightly against him, so tight he could feel her heart beating against his, or so it seemed.

Reaching around her, he shimmied the hem of her skirt up to her hips. The skin on her thighs was softer than the silk. When he found a lacy black pair of thong panties, he cursed. Undressing Ivy later was a treat he was going to savor. Though he yearned to strip her naked, he forced himself to find one last modicum of control.

His hands rested on her butt, although he kept them still.

His fingers itched to tangle in her hair and tilt her lips to his, but they both had to return to the dining room soon. She truly had blossomed since coming to Farrell's coastal hideaway. Any man would be lucky to have her, but that man wouldn't be Farrell. Soon, he would have some difficult decisions to make.

He kissed the side of her neck. "Do you know how special you are, Ivy? I've watched you this weekend. People love you. You're fun, and you get them to talk about themselves. You've made a huge contribution to Stone River Outdoors."

Ivy slipped her hands underneath his suit jacket and rubbed his back through his shirt. "Thank you for saying that. It's been great for me, too." She sighed. "We have to go back in there, Farrell. You know we do."

He squeezed her ass once, released her and stepped back. "I know. That's the hell of it."

Ivy smoothed her dress into place, checked her reflection in the mirror that hung over the fireplace and gave him the kind of smile women had been giving men for millennia. "Don't be so impatient, Farrell. We've got all night."

Sixteen

Ivy was not good at sneaking around. The one time she had tried ditching school for a day at the beach, her parents had found out and grounded her for a month. She was a *good* girl.

But look where it had gotten her. If she hadn't been such a people pleaser, she might have booted Richard to the curb long ago. Instead, she had tried to do the right thing. She had tried to make her marriage work.

In looking back, she realized it was never a marriage at all. Not in the truest sense of the word. She had been a prisoner of Richard's lies, her own grief and, ultimately, a deep-seated fear of being alone.

She wouldn't make those mistakes again. For one thing, Farrell had been completely clear about his inability to commit to a relationship. Ivy appreciated his honesty.

Going forward, she understood that she and Dolly were a family now. Whatever happened with Farrell was a pleasant blip in Ivy's life. Her job was to give her daughter a stable childhood, a happy home.

But tonight…

Ivy pinched her pale cheeks in the bathroom mirror. All she had to do was walk down the stairs nonchalantly. For all anyone knew, she might be getting a glass of milk.

The lovely, sophisticated nightwear Katie had picked out was the kind of thing Ivy had seen women wear in movies. The black satin gown slid over her skin like a caress, equally as comfortable as being nude, but even more provocative. Slit almost to her navel in front and to the base of her spine in back, it spelled out sex with every movement of her body.

The matching robe was also luxurious, but far more decorous, certainly modest enough to warrant a run-in with another guest without embarrassment for either party. She tightened the sash and knotted it firmly.

As it turned out, Ivy had worried for nothing. The house was still and quiet when she tiptoed down the main staircase and rounded the hall that led to Farrell's room. Not a soul stirred. Farrell's door was cracked, so she tapped lightly and entered.

A fire blazed in the hearth. The covers on the huge king bed were turned back. Farrell stood by the mantel, clad in nothing but a pair of low-slung navy knit sleep pants that left little to the imagination.

She sucked in a sharp breath and stopped, clinging to one of the bedposts when her knees wobbled and threatened to give out beneath her. "This looks cozy," she said, trying to sound like a woman of the world.

Farrell's grin warmed her cold toes. She had forgotten her slippers.

He crooked a finger. "Come by the fire, Ivy. Do you want a drink?"

"No, thanks." Alcohol at this hour would make her woozy. She didn't want to miss the good parts of what came next.

It struck her suddenly with a sharp stab of grief that she had been dead wrong. She'd told herself that spending time with Farrell was something she wanted, something she deserved. That when the clock ran out and she and Dolly moved on, Ivy would be able to look back on this interlude and be glad she had known and loved Farrell Stone even for a little while.

The truth ate at her now, destroying her illusions. In an instant, she realized that leaving this place—walking away from this complicated, kind, generous, amazing man—was going to destroy her.

Farrell must have seen something on her face. His smile faded. "What's wrong, Ivy?"

She swallowed hard. "Nothing. I'm just nervous." It wasn't entirely a lie. Her heart was beating like a jackhammer, and her teeth were in danger of chattering. Even her breathing was shaky.

Farrell didn't wait. He came to her. "Relax, Ivy. This night is for us. No pressure. Just pleasure." He slid his arms around her from behind and rested his chin on top of her head. "Earlier tonight you looked amazing in that red dress. But now, even better. Like a package I want to unwrap." His nimble fingers unknotted the tie at her waist.

She slipped out of her robe and tossed it on a chair, shored up by his strength and caring. "I want that, too."

"So glad we're on the same page." He chuckled hoarsely.

There wasn't much talking after that. Both of them had done a lot of "adulting" this weekend. Playing host. Working hard to make sure the event went smoothly.

It was time for self-indulgence.

Farrell picked her up and carried her to the bed. His hair was overdue for a cut, but the slightly shaggy look suited him. He was his own man, not bound by all of society's strictures. Though he was stunning in dress clothes, Ivy preferred this less-civilized version.

She wanted to tell him she loved him. Would it matter? Would it make a difference?

Maybe he wouldn't believe her. Maybe he'd say it was too soon after her marriage…that a rebound relationship wasn't the answer.

And maybe he would be forced to let her down gently, to remind her that Sasha had claimed his heart and still held it, even now.

Because Ivy didn't know the answers to those hypothetical scenarios, she kept quiet. Better to juggle uncertainty than to face the humiliation of an outright rejection, no matter how kind.

Farrell was impatient. She liked that. His urgency made her feel special. Desired. Desirable.

Though he had expressed appreciation for her new nightwear, he wasted no time in removing the gown. His knit pants joined the discarded lingerie. When they were both naked in the center of the mattress, he pulled the covers over them and dragged her against his warm body. His very warm body. The way his strong arms held her was delightful.

She ran her hands over his back, feeling the muscles, the taut flesh. "I was jealous of the Italian girl in your kayak," she admitted, her nose buried in his shoulder.

His chest rumbled with laughter. "Then we're even. Because I wanted to punch my brother for offering you lessons."

Farrell regretted the words as soon as they left his mouth. That admission made him sound more emotionally invested in this thing with Ivy than he wanted to admit.

She pulled back to stare at him. The only light in the room was a muted glow from the fireplace. "Are you serious?"

He shrugged. "Yeah. I thought we were all supposed to be taking one of the guests on board to show them the ropes. But then some of them wanted to go with their spouses, and suddenly Zachary ended up with you."

"Zachary is a wonderful man, but he's not Farrell Stone."

"What does that mean?"

"He's gorgeous and fun, but you're more like me, Farrell. You don't need a lot to be happy. Or that's how it seems to me. Am I wrong?"

Her assessment was startling. As if she really understood who he was. "He's always popular with women."

"You would be, too, if you didn't have this kind of
grumpy, standoffish thing going on." She paused, her
smile impish. "But I like you anyway, because you have
other *qualities* I find interesting."

When her hand closed around his erection, stroking
once...then twice, he inhaled sharply. "I see."

She handled him firmly, keeping him on the edge of
madness. "You're hardworking even though you have a
ridiculous amount of money. You're kind, though I suspect you'd rather not be described that way. And you've
given me a chance to get my life back with this job."

"I don't want your gratitude," he snapped. He heard
the bite in his own voice, but he couldn't help it. "What
we are...here...in this bed...doesn't have a damn thing
to do with kindness or gratitude or anything else. I want
you, Ivy. I need you. Do you understand?"

"Yes," she said softly. "I do."

He reached for protection, took care of business and
lifted her astride him. "I'm yours, Ivy. Show me what
you want."

Though shadows draped the bed in intimacy, he was
well able to see his lover's face. Her cute hair was mussed,
her cheeks stained pink with heightened color. His Ivy
was learning to be bold, to take and not simply give,
but her innate shyness lingered. When she rose up on
one knee and aligned their bodies, he literally couldn't
breathe. Everything in his chest froze, waiting for the
moment of joining. Waiting. Waiting.

Her body accepted his easily, though he was as hard

as he had ever been. His fingers gripped her hips, held her still, while he entered her. *Holy God.* His eyes stung with moisture. It was good. So good.

He'd never thought to find such closeness with a woman again.

And it terrified him. Clear down to the marrow of his bones. He felt stripped raw. Vulnerable.

Ivy's small, capable hands rested, palms flat, on his collarbone. She bent to kiss him. The change in position made them both gasp. "I want you," she whispered, her lips feathering over his with tiny angel-wing kisses. "For as long as we have. And I won't ask for more. So make love to me again and again, Farrell. Hard. Fast. Everything in between. I've got a lot of empty years to make up for. I need you, too."

He lost control then. Rolled her beneath him. Pounded his way to release. Gasped for air in the aftermath.

His bedroom was silent.

Ivy's heartbeat was loud. So was his.

The moment seemed right for some kind of confession on his part. Surely she realized that his self-imposed ban on caring was flimsy at best. But fear kept him silent.

After yawning twice, he kissed her shoulder. "Are you sleepy, Ivy? It's been a heck of a day."

She nodded, echoing his yawn with one of her own. "Yes. I'm going back upstairs now."

He scowled. "Why would you do that? It's two in the morning. Stay, Ivy. Stay here."

She patted his cheek like he was a fractious toddler demanding a treat. "I've decided I'd rather not take any chances with our guests. I'll be more comfortable in my own room."

When she rolled out of bed and bent to pick up her things, he was treated to a great view of her ass and her... He gave himself a metaphorical smack. "I could make you comfortable," he said, giving her a look that hopefully communicated his displeasure with this new plan.

Ivy donned the gown and robe and tied the sash. Her smile was weary and sweet. "I'll see you in the morning, Farrell. Get some sleep."

Ivy slept like the dead and awoke refreshed, even though she'd barely managed five hours. Last night had given her hope. Though perhaps it shouldn't have. Farrell had been so tender, so everything. Surely a man couldn't have sex like that without feeling *something*. Could he?

The morning passed quickly. After breakfast, guests returned upstairs to pack. The three Farrell men took turns transporting luggage to the front foyer. The limos were slated to arrive at two o'clock sharp to ferry everyone back to Portland. Zachary, Quin, Katie and Delanna would be heading that way, as well.

Soon, it would only be Farrell, Dolly and Ivy once again.

Ivy had missed her daughter, though Dolly had been having the time of her life with Delanna, who doted on her every move. Even though Ivy had been at the cabin for the baby's bedtime both nights, Dolly had clearly bonded with her weekend sitter.

While the Stone brothers and their guests were involved in one last short planning session after lunch, Katie and Ivy helped the caterer pack up her supplies. The woman had driven back and forth from Bar Harbor morning and night. Ivy hoped she was being paid well.

When the kitchen was spotless, Katie joined the meeting. Ivy ran upstairs to pack her own things. When she was done, she put the bag in the mudroom at the back of the house. Tonight she would return to her bed at the cabin. Farrell's plans were a mystery.

Not long afterward, everyone gathered on the porch for goodbyes. The group had bonded. Ivy liked them all. Delanna was there, too, carrying Dolly and getting in a few last snuggles.

Luca shocked Ivy by grabbing her up and giving her a more-than-friendly smack on the lips. His grin, when he released her, was unrepentant. "When you come to Switzerland, mademoiselle, you must find me and I will take you to dinner at the best restaurant in the world."

Ivy returned the smile, flattered in spite of the outrageous display. "I'll keep that in mind."

Quin and Katie joined her, laughing. "I think you made a new friend," Quin said, clearly joking.

Katie shushed him. "Don't tease." She squeezed Ivy's arm. "I know you wanted to save up money for a car, but Quin and I realized that my old sedan was sitting in the garage up here at his house gathering dust. Well, *our* house," she said, correcting herself. "You're welcome to it, if you like the way it drives. I put a lot of miles on it, but she's a good car."

Ivy stared at them. "You can't *give* me a car. I'll pay you."

Quin shook his head. "Your money is no good in Maine. I have more vehicles than I need, and I bought Katie a new Land Rover last month. You'd be doing us a favor by taking her old car off our hands." He reached in his pocket and handed Ivy a set of keys. "She's all yours. I'm sure Farrell can help you line up the title and tag transfer."

Farrell joined them, overhearing Quin's final words. He frowned. "Why does Ivy need a car?"

Katie's brows narrowed, telegraphing her displeasure with the man who was both her boss *and* her brother-in-law. "A woman should be independent. Ivy and Dolly need safe, reliable transportation."

"I have plenty of cars," Farrell said. He turned to Ivy. "If you wanted to borrow a car, all you had to do was ask."

Now Ivy was caught. She moved closer to Katie. "I told them I wanted to *buy* a car. They're offering me Katie's old one."

"You can have one of mine," he said. "For free."

Ivy could tell that he was serious. "I appreciate the offer," she muttered. "But since I work for you, it's probably less messy if I deal with Katie and Quin."

"Messy?" His eyes glittered.

She stared at him, daring him to make a scene. No one knew that Ivy and Farrell were lovers. She wanted to keep it that way. "Let's change the subject," she said. "Your guests are ready to go."

Farrell strode to the far side of the porch, leaving Katie and Quin to stare after him in disbelief.

Quin turned to Ivy. "What was that all about? He was pissed, and I didn't even do anything." His aggrieved expression was comical.

Katie, on the other hand, stared at Ivy as if her brain was doing calculations and perhaps coming up with the right answers.

Ivy gave them a big smile, hoping to derail Katie's suspicions. "Who knows? That brother of yours can be a bit of a curmudgeon." She glanced around, searching for a way out. "If you'll both excuse me, I need to say a few more goodbyes."

She talked to the Namibian couple, then exchanged email addresses with the Italian mother and father and the two daughters. One of the daughters handed Ivy a small tissue-wrapped parcel. "For your baby," she said shyly. "It's a doll I made from a handkerchief. My stitching is not very good."

Ivy unwrapped the package and smiled. It was the perfect toy for an inquisitive toddler. "I love it," she said. "Dolly will, too. *Grazie*."

The hired cars had pulled up adjacent to the base of the steps. Though the drivers exited and were standing by to receive their passengers, no one seemed in any particular hurry to go back to Portland.

Probably because the Stone brothers knew how to throw a party.

Zachary motioned for the drivers to collect the bags. Ivy moved in his direction and tried to pick up a carry-on or two. "I can help," she said.

"Not necessary, but thanks." He gave her a smile that was enough like his brother's to give her heart a squeeze.

The youngest of the drivers hefted three large suitcases, one in each hand and one under his arm, perhaps trying to impress the two Italian girls. When he swung around to descend the steps, the corner of a hard-sided bag bumped Ivy's hip. She stepped back instinctively to give the kid more room, but her foot found nothing but air.

She tried to regain her balance. It was too late.

The world turned upside down as she tumbled down the stairs.

Seventeen

Farrell was more than ready for everyone to be gone. He wanted his house to himself again. As he tried to usher people toward the transportation, he heard someone cry out. He spun on his heel, just in time to see Ivy fall down the steep front stairs.

His heart stopped. His feet refused to move. Fear paralyzed him. His vision narrowed, and for a moment, he felt as if he might pass out.

Dead. She could be dead.

Everyone surged en masse. Except Farrell. He tried to move, but his arms and legs felt uncoordinated, heavy. Zachary got to Ivy first. It wasn't until Farrell saw Ivy speaking to his brother that he was finally able to force himself down the steps.

Someone offered to call an ambulance. Farrell crouched

beside his lover. "No point," he said gruffly. "It would be an hour until someone gets here."

Zachary touched the bleeding scrape on Ivy's cheek. "He's right. My first-aid training is up-to-date. Let's evaluate her and make a decision."

Farrell nodded.

Ivy lifted an arm and waved her hand. "I'm right here. And I'm okay. It was my own clumsiness. I'll have bruises, but it's nothing serious."

"We'll be the judge of that." Farrell was curt.

Quin and Katie were having a whispered conference on the sidelines.

After Farrell and Zachary checked Ivy's arms and legs for broken bones, Farrell scooped her into his arms and moved carefully up the stairs, Zachary at his side. In the master suite, Farrell laid Ivy gently on his bed. The very same bed where he had lost himself in madness the night before.

Zachary checked her pulse. Examined her pupils. Barked out half a dozen questions. "Did you hit your head?" he asked urgently. "Tell us the truth."

"No," Ivy said forcefully. "I scraped my cheek on the corner of a step, but I don't even have a headache. My hip took the worst of it. Give me some ibuprofen, and I'll be fine. I need to get Dolly, so Delanna can leave."

Farrell stared at her, his heart still beating sluggishly. "Quin left with the group, because some of them had planes to catch. Katie stayed behind to look after the baby. Be still, damn it," he said when Ivy tried to get up.

She glared at him. "I know my own body. I'm not badly hurt."

Zachary shoved his hands in his pockets, his expression concerned. "Possibly. But we have to make sure you're not in shock. Farrell, you stay with her. I'll round up something for that wound."

Suddenly, silence descended. Ivy wouldn't look at him. Words he wanted to say hovered on his lips, but he choked them back. Sick to his stomach, he suddenly wanted to be anywhere but in this room.

Over and over in his head, he saw Ivy falling. Falling. Falling.

Zachary returned and cleaned Ivy's cheek. Then he added some antibiotic ointment and covered the deep scrape with a Band-Aid. "I don't think it will hurt to get it wet tonight. And you should sleep with it uncovered."

Ivy smiled. "Thanks, Zachary. I'm fine. Honest."

Farrell stared down at the bed. Why did Ivy look so impossibly small and defenseless? His heart turned over in his chest. What were these wild, tangled feelings that writhed inside him? He *didn't* love her. He was concerned. That was all.

"We'll let you rest," he said abruptly. He turned to his brother. "Let's find Katie and make a game plan."

In the kitchen, the three adults gathered. Katie grimaced. "Dolly is ready for her afternoon nap. What do you want me to do?"

Farrell paced, opened the fridge and extracted a beer. He downed half of it in two gulps. "Put the baby down in the study. Bring me the monitor. Then you and Zachary hit the road and see if you can catch up with the rest of the group. Quin will need help in Portland sorting everything out, because they're not all staying at the same hotel."

Zachary nodded. "Fair enough. And somebody—I can't remember who—is flying out tonight, not in the morning."

"I think it's Luca," Katie said. She held Dolly close, stroking her head. "Okay. I'll get this little one to sleep and say goodbye to Ivy. Zachary, let me know how soon you want to leave."

He glanced at his watch. "Fifteen minutes?"

"I'll meet you out front."

Farrell stared at Zachary. "Do you really think she's okay? I don't want this to be one of those stories where a concussion goes unnoticed."

"She says it was only her cheek. I don't see any signs to worry about. I've banged my head a time or two in the day, so I know the drill. But watch her for the next several hours."

"You can bet on it."

Ivy opened her eyes when the bedroom door creaked. Seeing Katie gave her a sigh of relief. For some reason, Farrell was acting weird. She couldn't handle that right now. Her whole body ached.

Katie came to the bed and perched on the edge of the mattress. "I just put Dolly down for her nap. Farrell has the monitor. Zachary and I are headed back to Portland to help Quin at the other end."

"I'm sorry I disrupted your plans for nothing."

Katie cocked her head. "Falling down an entire flight of steps isn't exactly nothing. Are you sure you don't need a hospital?"

"One-hundred-percent sure. I'm sore from head to toe, but no serious injuries. I'm a single mom. I won't do anything to endanger my health—I swear. Dolly needs me."

Katie stood and blew a kiss. "If you're sure." She paused. "Farrell is acting odd in all of this. Are you and he—"

Ivy interrupted quickly. "Farrell and I are nothing, Katie. He's my boss. Besides, you know how he is. The man is an enigma wrapped in a puzzle. Don't try to figure him out. You'll only frustrate yourself."

"I suppose."

Zachary hollered down the hall, clearly forgetting the sleeping baby.

"Gotta go. We'll talk soon. Bye, Ivy."

When the house was silent, Ivy eased out of bed. Farrell would be outside saying goodbye. In the bathroom, she glanced in the mirror and winced. Her hair was a mess, and she was paler than normal, not to mention the damage to her cheek.

Five minutes later when she returned, Farrell was leaning against one of the bedposts, arms crossed over his chest. A dark scowl gave him a menacing air. "I told you to stay in bed."

"I had to pee," she said, daring him to chastise her further. "I don't need a nanny, Farrell, though I appreciate your concern."

He shoved away from the bed and went to poke the fire. "Rest," he said bluntly. "I'll watch the monitor for the moment."

"That's not necessary." Something was off with Farrell. He seemed angry. But why? She went to him and put a hand on his shoulder. "You need to go back to the lab. I know you're itching to get to work on your project. I'm fine. I found medicine in your bathroom cabinet. As soon as it kicks in, I'll be almost good as new." She rested her cheek on his shoulder. "This was a fun weekend, but I'm glad everyone is gone."

His big frame stiffened. Noticeably. He shrugged out of her light embrace and headed for the door. "You're right," he muttered, not looking at her. "I do need to work. But I want you to text me every thirty minutes and let me know how you're doing."

Suddenly, she knew she was losing him, though she couldn't explain it. "Okay," she said slowly. "Would you like to come to the cabin for dinner tonight? Nothing fancy. After Dolly goes to sleep, we could…relax." She couldn't bring herself to say the *actual* words to describe sex. Not when he was being all aloof and weird.

Farrell never even turned to look at her. "I'll probably work late," he said. "And there are leftovers in the fridge. I'll see you tomorrow. Don't forget the texts."

Stunned, Ivy watched him walk out the door.

Three hours later, she was no closer to understanding what had happened. Her body felt awful, every bruise making itself known. But that was nothing compared to the ache in her chest. Her silly, foolish heart was beginning to crack into a million pieces.

As promised, she texted Farrell every thirty minutes to let him know she wasn't dead. The dark humor suited her mood.

Last night, Farrell had made love to her as if he would never let her go. Today, he could barely look at her. His on-again, off-again mood swings made her furious. And they hurt, too, but she concentrated on the anger. She loved the infuriating man—quite desperately, in fact. If she found the courage to tell him so, and the feelings were one-sided, she would have to leave.

Farrell didn't even try to sleep. He paced the confines of his small lab and searched for a way out. He didn't love Ivy. He didn't. The sick fear he experienced when he saw her tumble down his stairs was nothing more than concern for a friend, an employee.

The prospect that he *might* let himself get too involved galvanized him. He *couldn't* lose someone he loved again. He wouldn't allow it. If there was any possibility he might fall in love with Ivy, he had to step away from the madness now.

Even in the midst of his panicked rationalizations, he knew he was lying to himself. And he was ashamed of his cowardice. With every day that passed, Ivy had become more and more dear to him. Of course he loved her. How could he not?

He'd done a damn good job of denying it, though.

Seeing her fall down the stairs had revealed the depth of his love and also the impossibility of telling her how he felt.

He wanted her delectable body. That much was true. But it wasn't too late to stop himself from making a terrible mistake.

Every moment he'd spent in Ivy's bed and vice versa had been exquisitely pleasurable. Still, he had lived without physical release before. Months on end, in fact. He could deny himself. He had no other choice.

He had to let her go…

Ivy slept fitfully. Monday morning dawned gray and cold and blustery. It was as if the weather had stayed perfect for their out-of-town guests, and now that the party was over, Mother Nature was having a hissy fit.

Delanna had done a wonderful job caring for Dolly, but the cabin was a bit of a mess. Ignoring the aches and pains from her accident, Ivy did two loads of laundry while cleaning the place from top to bottom, thankful that Dolly was happily occupied with her pots and pans on the floor.

At ten thirty, Ivy decided to go to Farrell's house and make a plan for dinner. She had no idea what food was left. But she would throw something together that was better than reheating leftovers.

"Come on, lovey," she said to Dolly. "Let's take a walk." It wasn't actually raining at the moment, but she and Dolly bundled up for the short trek.

It seemed odd to find the big house empty and quiet after all the commotion of the weekend. But having the serene space was peaceful, too. Plenty of time to think.

With Dolly on her hip, she wandered into the kitchen. There on the counter, propped up with a banana, was an envelope with her name on it. She recognized Farrell's bold handwriting.

Something told her she wasn't going to like the contents. Why hadn't Farrell simply sent a text if he wanted something special? Or maybe he needed her to clean all the guest rooms, because he hadn't found anyone else to tackle the task.

After tucking Dolly in her high chair and giving her a handful of dry cereal, Ivy opened the note with shaking hands.

Ivy:

Now that the house party is over and my project is wrapping up, I think it's best if you return to Portland. Because this change is somewhat sooner than you expected, I am including a severance check, as well as a letter of reference.

I plan to be at the house by two this afternoon. I'll help you pack up. We'll drive my SUV back to Portland, so the high chair and port-a-crib will fit. Feel free to text Katie if you need her to do anything on the other end.

F.

Ivy stared at the piece of paper, trying to decipher the words. *Sooner than you expected. Severance.*

And not even his whole name. Just "F."

She felt sick. Betrayed. Stunned. He had told her from the beginning that he wouldn't allow his feelings to be involved. It wasn't Farrell's fault that she hadn't believed him.

Anger would have helped. She tried to be angry. She *wanted* to be angry like she had been before. But her body was literally battered and bruised, and now her spirit was in equal pain.

Had Farrell somehow decided she was going to cling or make demands? Had he thought it best to end their short-lived affair before things got messy?

Tears stung her eyes, but she didn't let them fall.

Every paycheck she had earned sat in her purse down at the cabin. The severance amount in her hand was humiliating, but she didn't have the luxury of shredding it and leaving the pieces on the counter.

So she did what every survivor has always done. She picked up her child, and she walked out.

Farrell paced the confines of his Portland office, wanting to smash things. Both of his brothers and Katie sat nearby, watching him with sympathy in their eyes. That compassion ate at him, because those were the same expressions he had received from *everyone* when Sasha died.

He had hated it then, and he hated it now. Those looks meant that his life was screwed. Destroyed. Over.

For five solid weeks he had searched for Ivy and Dolly. But they had vanished from the face of the earth. Finally, in despair, he realized he needed help. So he had summoned his family and told them everything.

"When she had the accident on the stairs," he croaked, remembering that terrible day, "it was like having everything click into sharp focus. I understood that I was falling in love with her, and I was terrified."

Quin sighed. "So you decided to get rid of her."

Farrell winced. "I couldn't go through that again. Losing someone. Ivy could have died on those steps."

"But she didn't," Zachary said. "And now you've lost her anyway."

Farrell sucked in a breath, his chest heaving. Zachary was right. Farrell had made a terrible mistake, and he had to fix it. "You have to help me find her," Farrell said. "Please. She didn't even take all the baby's things."

Katie stood and went to the window, her face drawn with worry. "As a female, I can only imagine what she's going through. A woman like Ivy wouldn't offer her body easily. She must have cared for you, Farrell. But knowing Ivy, she would have kept those feelings to herself, because she believes you still love Sasha."

"Why would she think that?" he bellowed, half-frantic with panic.

Quin put an arm around his shoulders. "Because we all thought that, Farrell. Until Ivy, you've not looked at a woman seriously in seven years. Ivy would have no way of knowing that you cared. Not without the words, especially since you sent her away."

Zachary's jaw firmed. "We'll find her, I swear. What ground have you covered so far?"

"I started in the Charleston area. Two weeks with a private investigator. All we managed to prove was that she hadn't been back since she came north and moved in with Delanna. So I returned here to Portland. I've combed every apartment complex in the city. Twice. I even had a buddy of mine at the DMV try to trace the registry on that car you gave her." He glared at Quin and Katie, though he knew who was really to blame for Ivy's flight.

Katie turned and gave all three men a look of disgust. "Think it through. Ivy would rather risk getting a ticket than having Farrell find her. She probably didn't register the car."

The truth of that struck Farrell like a death blow to the gut. What had he done? Good God, what had he done?

"So what next?" he groaned. "It's a big damn country."

"Bar Harbor," Katie said, her face beginning to reflect hope. "When I first drove Ivy and Dolly up to your house, we passed the turnoff for Bar Harbor. Ivy mentioned that she had always wanted to spend some time there. Her family visited Acadia briefly when she was a kid, and she was fascinated by the park."

Quin nodded. "It's no better or worse than any other idea."

Zachary drummed his fingers on the desk, his serious expression far from the carefree facade he typically showed to the world. He sat in Farrell's chair making notes. "It's tricky, but I could get someone to trace her Social Security number."

"Won't work," Katie said. "If a woman wants to hide, she'll get a job that pays cash."

Farrell straightened his spine. "Then Bar Harbor it is. If necessary, I'll sell part of my shares in SRO to both of you to finance this search."

Quin rolled his eyes. "Don't be an asshole, big brother. And don't insult us. If Ivy is important to you, we're in on this. One hundred percent."

Eighteen

Ten days of searching the Bar Harbor area, and Farrell
was so tired he was weaving on his feet. He'd barely
managed three or four hours of sleep a night for weeks.
Shame and regret and dread ate away at the lining of
his stomach. It was torture to imagine Ivy laboring all
alone to support herself and her child.

He loved that stubborn, precious woman, and he'd
never told her. He'd let his fear drive her away. Among
all the other reasons that kept him searching was the
need to apologize. To tell her how he felt. And regard-
less of the outcome, to beg her forgiveness.

When she disappeared, she had left the baby bed.
The high chair. Every last item of couture wardrobe
Katie had helped pick out.

The woman who fled an abusive marriage and came

north to Maine for a new start had left Farrell's home with little more than the clothes on her back.

Because he had hurt her. Badly.

Now, at last, he was about to confront his mistakes. At least he hoped so. True to their word, Zachary and Quin and Katie had committed all their time and effort to locating a woman who didn't want to be found.

Even in a relatively small community like Bar Harbor, those searches had taken time.

Now it was up to Farrell. He stared at the tiny, run-down motel from the anonymity of a rental car. The rental was to keep Ivy from spotting him and running again.

The Summer's Beauty Inn was anything but. Beautiful, that was. It was the kind of place that might have been a popular tourist haunt in the 1950s. Now it existed far off the beaten path, slowly decaying into the surrounding hillside.

Katie's familiar sedan, now Ivy's, sat in front of the unit marked 7E. The car was backed into the spot, so there was no way to tell if it had a license tag.

Farrell only knew that his quest was just beginning.

He wasn't a praying man, not particularly, but he muttered a few words of supplication in hopes that a benevolent deity might take pity on him. Or maybe Sasha might intervene on his behalf. Farrell would take any help he could get at this point.

When he glanced at his watch, he marked the hour. Six fifteen. Early enough that Dolly wouldn't be asleep. Late enough that the two females who held his heart might have eaten.

Farrell's appetite had been nonexistent for weeks.

He gathered his phone and his keys and climbed out of the car. The twenty steps toward the door with the peeling green paint felt like a marathon. What could he say to make things right?

Even worse, what if those words didn't exist?

Ivy flinched when someone knocked at her door. Old habit. She'd had a few drunken losers try to get in the wrong room since she had been here.

When she looked out the peephole, she moaned and put her back to the door, clutching Dolly to her chest. No. No. No.

She stayed perfectly still, heart pounding, mouth dry.

Farrell's deep voice accompanied a second round of knocking. "I know you're in there, Ivy. Open up."

He couldn't possibly know for sure. Of course, her car was out front. Katie's car, actually. Ivy was going to pay for it, just not yet. Living expenses were eating through her stash of money at an alarming rate.

Dolly, unaware that she was supposed to be quiet, started babbling. The little girl was becoming more vocal every day. Ivy was proud of her daughter, but now was not the time. "Ssh, sweetheart."

Silence reigned for one minute. Then two. Then three. Maybe Farrell had given up.

The fact that Ivy's first response to that possibility was disappointment meant she was in deep doo-doo.

If she peered out the peephole again, would he be able to see her eyeball? She'd never considered what it looked like from the other side of the door. But she was desperate to know if he was still there.

Sliding the drapes aside wasn't an option. The Farrell she knew would jump on that immediately.

If he hadn't walked away.

Before she could make up her mind, a small white business card slid under the door. It was Farrell's, of course. All of his various Stone River Outdoors info was on one side. But when she flipped the card over, there were only two words—*I'm sorry...*

Her eyes stung. It didn't really matter, did it? Not in the big scheme of things. But if he wasn't going to leave, she had to deal with him.

All she had to do was hold it together for fifteen or twenty minutes. He would salve his conscience. She would absolve him. Then they would go their separate ways.

Could she bear it? She had missed him so badly, only sheer exhaustion allowed her to sleep. She dreamed about him. Every night.

She'd walked out of his cabin almost seven weeks ago and into the current, temporary arrangement. She was working toward a bigger plan. Once she had a decent nest egg for first and last months' rent and utility deposits, she hoped to rent a nice apartment in Portland. Jobs would be more plentiful there and not dependent on the vagaries of the tourist season.

She wasn't alone in the world. She had made friends with Katie and Delanna. Eventually, one or both of them could be the beginning of her new community, her circle of emotional support. But she hadn't contacted either of them yet. She hadn't wanted to chance having word of her whereabouts get back to Farrell. He couldn't have been too upset, though, if it had taken him this long to show up. Why was he here?

In her heart, she knew why. He was a decent man, and he knew he had hurt her feelings. That was all she would admit to... No reason for him to know how she really felt. No reason at all.

"I need you to be a cute distraction," she whispered to Dolly. The little girl slobbered and blew a bubble and tooted. Great. So much for backup.

The next knock sounded fiercer. "Open the door, Ivy."

Dear God, please don't let me make a fool of myself.

She looked down at her faded jeans and her long-sleeved navy Henley top. The casual clothes were a far cry from the beautiful wardrobe she had worn for the weekend retreat. Not to mention that she had a smear of mashed banana on her sleeve and a tiny hole at her elbow.

Cinderella was definitely back with the mice.

Before she could lose her nerve, she smoothed her hair with one hand and jerked open the door. "Hello, Farrell. What brings you here?"

Farrell had almost given up. If Ivy didn't want to see him, did he *have* to leave, or could he try to make amends? While he was still wrestling with that thorny question, there she was.

"Ivy..." His words dried up.

She stepped back. "Come in."

The motel room was dismal. That was the nicest description he could come up with. Ivy herself was everything he remembered and more. The hazel eyes with the wary gaze. Pointed chin. Unpainted pink lips that had kissed him and offered him joy again. He wanted to grab her and hold her and never let her go.

But even a blind man could sense the great chasm between them.

He cleared his throat. "I couldn't find you."

She frowned. "I'm only an hour from your house... give or take."

"Don't be coy. You hid in plain sight. I've been to Charleston for two weeks. And all over Portland. You didn't register the car, damn it." He was losing it, and Ivy's expression closed up.

She pursed her lips. "I'm sorry you've been inconvenienced, Farrell. But I'm not sure what that has to do with me."

He glanced behind him at the two beds. Both were covered with bilious green satin bedspreads that matched the door. "May we please sit down?"

She shrugged. "If you like."

Dolly was giving him the stink eye. Didn't the kid remember how many times he had played with her? Sung to her? Rubbed her back as she fell asleep?

An awkward silence fell. Where to start...

Ivy glanced at her watch.

Farrell decided to cut to the chase. "I'm not in love with Sasha anymore, I swear. She was my first love. And I will always honor her memory, but she's my past."

Ivy blinked. "Okay."

The stubborn woman wasn't going to make this easy on him.

He didn't really blame her. So he took a breath and kept going.

"I'm sorry I threw you out," he said. "That was cowardly. And wrong."

Another blink. "Got it. No worries."

"Please come back with me," he begged.

This time her eyes flashed fire, a fire he hadn't fully understood until this moment. "No, thank you," she said, her tone excruciatingly polite. "Dolly and I are fine."

"Do you even have a job?" he asked in desperation. "We tried tracing your Social Security number, but nothing pinged."

"We?" Her facade cracked. "Who's *we*?"

"Zachary and Katie and Quin, of course. I needed help finding you. So I told them everything."

Her eyes widened. "No."

He shrugged. "Yes. Not the intimate details, of course, but enough to give them a clear picture of the urgency I felt."

This time, she frowned. "What urgency?"

He took a deep breath. "I told them I loved you, but that I had treated you badly and made you run away."

Ivy went so white he thought she might pass out. The mostly-healed scrape on her cheek was visible still. She was far too thin. Had she not been eating well?

"Yes, you did," she said, her lips pale. "But I've pursued other employment."

"What do you do?" He didn't really care, but he

sensed he needed to keep the conversation flowing or she would shut him down.

Ivy played with Dolly's hair. "I wait tables at a bar six nights a week. My shift starts at nine and ends at one in the morning. The lady next door comes here to my room and watches TV while Dolly sleeps. The bar tips are decent. I give her part of my paycheck for her trouble."

Good God. That meant Ivy was wandering the streets in the middle of the night, vulnerable to any number of dangers.

And all because of him. He hadn't thought his spirits could sink any lower. It wasn't so easy to speak casually this time, because his throat was tight with emotion. "When do *you* sleep?" he muttered.

Ivy stared at him. "From two until seven in the morning, when this little one wakes up. And again during her naps. It's not so bad. We're making it work."

Farrell looked around him at the awful orange-and-gold wallpaper and the threadbare carpet with the unidentifiable stains. He wanted to cry. And he would have if he thought Ivy would take pity on him.

Why should she ever forgive him for what he had done? At least her bastard of a husband had kept a roof over her head. Farrell had made her homeless. He swallowed hard.

"Did you hear what I said earlier?"

"About what?"

"I told Katie and Quin and Zachary that I loved you."

Her bottom lip trembled. "But you never told me."

Huge tears welled in her eyes, rolled down her cheeks, wet the baby's head.

"Ah, God, Ivy." He went to her, his heart breaking, and knelt beside the bed. Taking her free hand in his, he kissed it, held it to his cheek. "I love you, Ivy Danby. You burst into my world, not like a blazing comet, but like a quiet, unremarkable moon on the back side of a planet. I barely knew you were there at first, and then I started looking for you. All the time."

The hint of a smile interrupted her tears. "That's a terrible metaphor, Farrell. Stick to inventing."

"I'm pretty sure it's a simile, but we can argue about that later." He looked up at her, letting her see the nights of agonized worry, the deep regret, the unquenchable hope. "I adore you, Ivy. I knew it when I made love to you that last night, but I thought I could keep my emotions out of it. Then you fell down those god-awful steps, and I realized how easily I could lose you. It terrified me. I didn't want to feel that pain again. So I shoved you away."

He laid his cheek on her thigh. "I am so sorry, my love. Sorrier than you will ever know. Forgive me for being such a complete and utter failure as a human being."

Slender fingers sifted through his hair. His heart stopped. Jerked. Beat again more rapidly.

Ivy exhaled, a broken, shaky sound that heaped more coals of fire on his head. "I forgive you, Farrell. I do. And I even understand. But I'm not the woman to replace your Sasha."

Farrell stood abruptly and lifted Dolly from Ivy's

arms. He grabbed the baby's favorite stacking cups from the dresser and set her and the toy in the port-a-crib. A brand-new one. He patted the baby's head. "Give me ten minutes, Dolly. Please. And if we've got a deal, I'll buy you a pony on your fifth birthday."

Luckily for him, the little girl was in a mood to be entertained easily.

Farrell spun back toward the bed, took Ivy's cold hands in his and drew her to her feet. He squeezed her fingers, looking down into her glorious hazel eyes. "Listen to me, Ivy. You're *nobody's* replacement. Ever. You're not second-string. You're not the consolation prize. You're strong and brave and tough and vulnerable. I love everything about you. When you were in a bad situation, you fought your way through, and you made it. You kept yourself and your daughter afloat against all odds."

She shook her head slowly. Nothing in her expression told him she had heard or believed a word he said. "You don't have to rescue me, Farrell. I've rescued myself. I'm only here at the motel temporarily. I have several job interviews coming. I've made plans for the future, for Dolly and me. I enjoyed having sex with you. A lot. But I'm moving on."

"Don't lie to me, sweetheart. I was there. You gave me your precious body and you took mine as your right. We were *together* in every sense of the word. You're my future, Ivy. I can't live without you. I won't. If I have to, I'll book the room next door and wait up for you every night until you come home to me. You're mine, Ivy. I didn't know it would happen like this, and God knows, I don't deserve you, but if you'll give me another chance, you won't ever have reason to doubt me again."

He ran out of breath and out of words.

Only their hands touched.

Ivy's big-eyed gaze searched his face. He wasn't sure what she saw. He'd been torn apart and put back together so many times in these past weeks, he wasn't the same man. "Ivy?"

She reached up slowly, put her hands on his cheeks, tested the stubble on his chin, stroked his brow. "You mean it, don't you?"

He nodded, willing her to understand. "I've never felt like this before. I was a very young man when I was with Sasha. We were young together, and we were naive about what the world could throw at us. But you and I have been through hell and back, Ivy. We've been tested, tried. Neither of us knows what the future holds, but I will love you for as many days as we have on this earth, and I pray they'll be too many to count."

She sniffed and wiped her nose on his expensive Egyptian cotton shirt. "Engineers aren't supposed to be poets." She wrapped her arms around his neck and clung. "I love you, too. Almost since the beginning. And I won't let you go either."

Her admission sent a shudder through his body, a wave of pained relief. For the longest time, they stood there, wrapped in each other's arms, contemplating how close they had come to having nothing at all. At last, Farrell couldn't bear it anymore. He pulled back, found her lips with his and kissed her. Until they were both dizzy.

He ran his thumb over her soft cheek. "You're my world, Ivy. You and Dolly."

Her eyes sparkled. "And you're the best man I've ever known. I want to be your wife, please."

"Is that a proposal?" he asked, chuckling at her artless assurance.

The woman in his arms gave him a look that warmed all the cold places in his heart. "Take me home, Farrell, to your cabin in the woods. It's where all good fairy tales start. We'll live happily ever after."

"You can bet on it, my love. You can bet on it."

* * * * *

Zachary Stone is determined to lay his family's problems to rest. When the one person who can help him turns out to be his former rival, he is torn between duty and desire.

He's the last bachelor among the Men of Stone River. Has he met his match?

Don't miss Zachary's story

Secrets of a Playboy

Available July 2020!

COMING NEXT MONTH FROM

⊞ HARLEQUIN

DESIRE

Available July 7, 2020

#2743 BLACK SHEEP HEIR
Texas Cattleman's Club: Rags to Riches • by Yvonne Lindsay
Blaming the Wingate patriarch for her mother's unhappiness, Chloe Fitzgerald wants justice for her family and will go through the son who left the fold—businessman Miles Wingate. But Miles is not what she expected, and the white-hot attraction between them may derail everything...

#2744 INSATIABLE HUNGER
Dynasties: Seven Sins • by Yahrah St. John
Successful analyst Ryan Hathaway is hungry for the opportunity to be the next CEO of Black Crescent. But nothing rivals his unbridled appetite for his closest friend, Jessie Acosta, when he believes she's fallen for the wrong man...

#2745 A REUNION OF RIVALS
The Bourbon Brothers • by Reese Ryan
After ending a sizzling summer tryst years ago, marketing VP Max Abbott doesn't anticipate reuniting with Quinn Bazemore—until they're forced together on an important project. He's the last person she wants to see, but the stakes are too high and so is their chemistry...

#2746 ONE LAST KISS
Kiss and Tell • by Jessica Lemmon
Working with an ex isn't easy, but successful execs Jayson Cooper and Gia Knox make it work. That is until they find themselves at a wedding where one kiss leads to one hot night. But will secrets from their past end their second chance?

#2747 WILD NASHVILLE WAYS
Daughters of Country • by Sheri WhiteFeather
Country superstar Dash Smith and struggling singer Tracy Burton were engaged—until a devastating event tore them apart. Now all he wants to do is help revive her career, but the chemistry still between them is too hard to ignore...

#2748 SECRETS OF A PLAYBOY
The Men of Stone River • by Janice Maynard
To flush out the spy in his family business, Zachary Stone hires a top cyber expert. When Frances Wickersham shows up, he's shocked the quiet girl he once knew is now a beautiful and confident woman. Will she be the one to finally change his playboy ways?

HDCNM0620

"Everyone is here," Max said. "Who are we—"

"I apologize for the delay. I got turned around on my way back from the car."

Max snapped his attention in the direction of the familiar voice. He hadn't heard it in more than a decade, but he would never, *ever* forget it. His mouth went dry, and his heart thudded so loudly inside his chest he was sure his sister could hear it.

"Peaches?" He scanned the brown eyes that stared back at him through narrowed slits.

"Quinn." She was gorgeous, despite the slight flare of her nostrils and the stiff smile that barely got a rise out of her dimples. "Hello, Max."

The "good to see you" was notably absent. But what should he expect? It was his fault they hadn't parted on the best of terms.

Quinn settled into the empty seat beside her grandfather. She handed the old man a worn leather portfolio, then squeezed his arm. The genuine smile that lit her brown eyes and activated those killer dimples was firmly in place again.

He'd been the cause of that magnificent smile nearly every day that summer between his junior and senior years of college when he'd interned at Bazemore Orchards.

"Now that everyone is here, we can discuss the matter at hand."

His father nodded toward his admin, Lianna, and she handed out bound presentations containing much of the info he and Molly had reviewed that morning.

"As you can see, we're here to discuss adding fruit brandies to the King's Finest Distillery lineup. A venture Dad, Max and Zora have been pushing for some time now." Duke nodded in their general direction. "I think the company and the market are in a good place now for us to explore the possibility."

Max should be riveted by the conversation. After all, this project was one he'd been fighting for the past thirty months. Yet it took every ounce of self-control he could muster to keep from blatantly staring at the beautiful woman seated directly across the table from him.

Peaches. Or rather, Quinn Bazemore. Dixon Bazemore's granddaughter. She was more gorgeous than he remembered. Her beautiful brown skin looked silky and smooth.

The simple, gray shift dress she wore did its best to mask her shape. Still, it was obvious her hips and breasts were fuller now than they'd been the last time he'd held her in his arms. The last time he'd seen every square inch of that shimmering brown skin.

Zora elbowed him again and he held back an audible *oomph*.

"What's with you?" she whispered.

"Nothing," he whispered back.

So maybe he wasn't doing such a good job of masking his fascination with Quinn. He'd have to work on the use of his peripheral vision.

Max opened his booklet to the page his father indicated. He was thrilled that the company was ready to give their brandy initiative a try, even if it was just a test run for now.

It was obvious why Mr. Bazemore was there. His farm could provide the fruit for the brandy. But that didn't explain what on earth Quinn Bazemore—his ex—was doing there.

Don't miss what happens next in
A Reunion of Rivals by Reese Ryan.

Available July 2020 wherever
Harlequin Desire books and ebooks are sold.

Harlequin.com